Praise for DON'T PITY THE DESPERATE

Myra is in deep trouble, exactly the sort of trouble American teens find themselves in, here in the centerless middle of endless suburbia, of late stage capitalism, driven by longings she cannot control or decipher. In a voice that rises up out of her deepest insecurities and denials, DON'T PITY THE DESPERATE tracks Myra's progress toward her own truth, or at least a self that is by degrees more survivable, and there is much bravery and beauty in the telling. This deep-hearted, penetrating portrait delivers the thing I want most in any story: the feeling that the writer's life depended, at least a little, in getting it on the page.

—**Pam Houston, author of** *Deep Creek* **and** *Finding Hope in the High Country*

From page one, DON'T PITY THE DESPERATE is riveting, encompassing the grief, confusion and, yes, the desperate wanting of a young addict named Myra who has lost her way. Deadpan, darkly humorous and profoundly touching, Moore's novel is full of knife-sharp insights about rehabs and recovery – and I fear those insights are as true today as they were in the 1980s, when this story is set. Is recovery possible? And what, exactly, are we recovering from? Vivid and evocative, Moore's story is unforgettable. It lingers in my imagination still.

—**Samantha Dunn, Author of** *Failing Paris* **and** *Not By Accident: Reconstructing a Careless Life*

An unsparing examination of the kids who use and the imperfect program designed to save them, this novel spares the reader nothing. In prose that is razor sharp yet dazzlingly beautiful, Anna B. Moore probes "the spot between feeling and truth," stirring hope and compassion for us all. A riveting debut.

—**Rob Davidson, author of** *Welcome Back to the World: A Novella and Stories*

Moore has written a beautiful vault of truths.

—**Josh Mohr, author of** *Model Citizen* **and** *Damascus*

In beautiful, harrowing, and often funny prose, Anna Moore's DON'T PITY THE DESPERATE knits together all the feelings and realities of trying to emerge from addiction– the pathos, the gallows humor, the family difficulties, the regeneration of self – into a compulsively readable novel constructed of lovely sentences and electric scenes. Moore builds the book's central character, Myra, with such a deft hand, with such nuance, delicacy, and believability. Moore's dialogue and secondary characters pull you from page to page, each remarkably vivid and each its own whole world. You will root for Myra at every stage of her journey. A truly compelling, moving, and well-crafted look at the complexities of recovery.

—**Amy Stuber, author of** *Sad Grownups*

Moore has written a book that uncannily and stunningly gets inside the mind of a teenager struggling with loss, identity, self-worth, confusion, doubt, and hormones–all while in rehab. As a reader, we are both rooting for Myra and remembering when we were Myra, with all the swirling issues of adolescence on top of life itself. It's beautiful, tender, and tough all at the same time—mirroring the subject she so deftly writes about.

—**J.J. Elliott, author of** *There Are No Words For This*

Moore's kaleidoscopic look at the pain and confusion of early recovery is unapologetically raw and unfiltered. In its conflicted portrayal of the teen rehab experience and the challenges of surrender, DON'T PITY THE DESPERATE reflects on absence, trauma, desire, and desperation, all within the fluid and chaotic state of adolescent identity. The center of this novel is a triad of questions every addict has asked: What would it be like to feel less alone? Is there a God? And what would it take to choose life?

—**Tara Stillions Whitehead, author of** *They More Than Burned* **and** *The Year of the Monster*

Anna B Moore has the rare, remarkable ability to embody young characters with authenticity and intensity. You open DON'T PITY THE DESPERATE and are instantly immersed, immediately drawn into what is real and true in the lives of these almost-adults. Moore opens a window into the world of teen recovery, a world many don't know much about, and she writes with precision and compassion. There is such love in these pages, such care for these kids. By the end, I was profoundly changed by Myra's story, and by all of the complicated people who'd come so alive on the page.

—**Hannah Grieco, editor** *of Already Gone: 40 Stories of Running Away* **and** *And If That Mockingbird Don't Sing: Parenting Stories Gone Speculative*

DON'T PITY THE DESPERATE
Copyright © 2024 ANNA B. MOORE
All Rights Reserved.
Published by Unsolicited Press.
First Edition.

No part of this book may be used or reproduced in any manner whatsoever without written permission except in the case of brief quotations embodied in critical articles or reviews. People, places, and notions in these stories are from the author's imagination; any resemblance to real persons or events is purely coincidental.

For information contact:
Unsolicited Press
Portland, Oregon
www.unsolicitedpress.com
orders@unsolicitedpress.com
619-354-8005

Cover Art: René Bouchard
Cover Design: Kathryn Gerhardt
Editor: S.R. Stewart

ISBN: 978-1-963115-21-5

I am grateful for the following programs, places, and people:

Writing by Writers DRAFT! Program, where I found renewed hope for the book after ignoring it in an extended fit of political and creative despair. Samantha Dunn, Pam Houston, Joshua Mohr, and Karen Nelson—thank you. To all the DRAFTers I continue to learn so much from, who have supported my book like mad: Pam Ferdinand, Stephany Wilkes, Quinn White, Simi Monheit, Elle Johnson, Ellie Rodgers, Betsy Stone, Jen Cowan Parsons, Suzanne Lewis, Liz Tucker, Anne Scott, and Michaela Haas —thank you.

Hannah Grieco, whose direction and knowledge I don't know where I would be without—thank you.

René Bouchard, whose artistry and universal amazingness inspires me every day—thank you.

J.J. Elliott, Amy Stuber, Tara Stillions Whitehead, and Rob Davidson, who so graciously supported my book—thank you.

Slow Theatre in Chico, CA, who put on a reading for me early in the process of my writing this book, with fabulous teen actors playing the characters—thank you.

Grin City Collective in Grinnell, Iowa, where I wrote like a machine and breathed the manicured Iowa landscape. Molly Rideout—thank you.

The first set of writers who saw and supported the manuscript: Bonnie Pape, Hilary Tellesen, and Beth Spencer—thank you.

The Abbey of our Lady of New Clairvaux, where on a retreat I finally, finally threw myself into the novel-writing process—thank you.

Unsolicited Press, whose acceptance of my book means that I find myself achieving something I did not think I could do—thank you for all you do for writers and readers everywhere.

To teenagers: glorious, brilliant, devastating. We fail you. We forget. I'm sorry.

Contents

MEANINGFUL THINGS	13
BABY BIRDS	24
NORMALCY	32
SPINS	35
PLEDGE	49
TRUTHFULNESS	52
FEAR	60
DISSENT	65
ADAPTING	68
VERACITY	78
PLANS	80
BOYS, CRYING	96
DEPARTURE	102
FREEDOM	110
PERFORMANCE PART 1	113
PERFORMANCE PART 2	121
DAMAGE	128
ANXIETY	134
CONSEQUENCES	136
FAITH	144

SYSTEMS	146
CONVERSION	151
CYCLES	166
SENDOFFS	178
MOM	186
ARTIFICE	191
MORALS	202
STEP FIVE	210
GRADUATION	213

Don't Pity the Desperate

Meaningful Things

Myra would tell the Community about the cat. It was the first thing she remembered anyway, a black blob moving across the gravel road. She saw it in a blink and then it was under the Nova's wheel.

"You can go faster than *that*," Chad had kept saying, his voice low and lovely from the backseat. He'd said he was too tired from baseball practice to sit up front with her. She knew she shouldn't accept this but did anyway and felt herself relinquishing something, giving up and in.

She could see in the rearview his soft chin, his brown curls. She wanted to touch his face, run her fingers along the sides of his nose, across his cheekbones. She was finally alone with him, with Chad Norris, with nobody else. She popped open the can of Budweiser he handed her and put it between her legs and pushed the clutch in and shifted the Nova to third and zoomed up the tiny hill at forty miles per hour, dust swirling up from the gravel.

"Right on, Myra!" Chad called.

Myra smiled and flipped her hair back, then saw the cat and felt the bump.

"Oh my God," she said. She stopped the car. "Was that a cat?"

"Oh well," Chad said.

"What if it's still alive?" Myra shifted into reverse.

"What are you doing?" Chad asked.

"Going back."

"I mean with that." He pointed to the gearshift, a lever on the steering column.

"This is a really old Nova from the seventies. You shift on the steering column."

"No way."

"Yep. Three on the tree."

Chad laughed—she had made him laugh—and opened another Budweiser. After Myra had picked him up from baseball practice, he asked her to stop at the *ampm* on Highway 6 so he could buy beer. He knew the checker, he said. Myra watched him walk inside and left the engine running because if she turned it off it might not start again, and this was embarrassing and stupid and Myra would do nothing to interfere with the progression of this night.

"You killed it. Don't worry," he said. "Don't go back."

"What if it's crying by the side of the road?"

"Did you feel that bump? It's dead." He leaned back in the muck of her father's junk in the backseat.

"I'm going back."

"What are you going to do if it's almost dead? Kill it?"

"I don't know." The Nova's engine rumbled. It runs, her father said. That's all a car needs to do. You'd think Myra might be embarrassed by such a car, but everyone thought it was funny. It made them all recognize her and know who she was.

"There's more beer at my house. Let's go."

She had been dreaming about Chad for weeks, the new boy who had moved to Iowa City from Solon and become her partner in advanced biology and a figure of worship in two of her other classes. Chad eased her ache for Mark, who, since dumping her for being psycho, no longer went to her locker between classes or called her every night or ever. When she did see him, Myra stared while he pretended she was not there. That they had never dated. That she had never been his escort during the Homecoming King and Queen Nomination Ceremony. That he had never told her he loved her in the front seat of his Trans Am, the night soft all around them while they listened to "Every Breath You Take." That he had never come while they humped on his basement sofa. That he had never brought her a rose.

But now Myra ached for Chad—his body and his eyes but mostly for his hands touching her face, her breasts, her hips, her back, her self, and her desires that were all so overwhelming and limitless that Myra was left ashamed.

"We could go to One Tree and drink some beer," he said. "It's over the hill."

Myra made sure Chad wasn't watching and twirled a few strands of hair from her scalp at the base of her neck, then yanked. She brushed the ends against her collarbone, a whisper on her skin.

She shifted to drive.

They hadn't even made out at One Tree—a raised concrete slab set back from the road beneath a giant weeping willow that hung low to the ground. The slab was cool through Myra's jeans. Cows mooed in the distance. Silhouettes of houses or barns or whatever other buildings were out here dotted the horizon, which she could see in the lights from Iowa City.

"It's so quiet," Myra had said.

Those trees in the distance—were they maple trees? Weren't there a lot of maple trees out in the country? Their leaves were bigger than giant hands and pointed, but these were the only facts she knew about them; most trees Myra did not recognize. She knew the names of almost nothing in the biological world even though she had always tried to learn because flowers, trees, shrubs, leaves, and grasses—knowing what they were and where they were and how they changed as they grew—was key to something important about existence. But still she could never retain the information, even when she designed her own quizzes. She had failed every one of them and so failed at being who she wanted to be, and she felt this failure all the time.

"Yep," Chad said.

Myra dangled her feet, opened another beer, lit a cigarette—but she was careful not to move much or talk much so nothing could get ruined. She would be quiet, nice, smiley, sweet. She waited to see what he would want, crossing her toes instead of her fingers. She didn't believe in God, but she started to pray. She had never felt so powerless.

***

This was the night she had to tell them about. She knew that most of the Community's responses would be gentle. *Glad you're here. Thanks for sharing.* If someone was in denial, the responses were a little harsher but grounded in concern: *I'm scared for you, man.*

Myra's primary counselor was named Rachel, and in Small Group therapy every morning and afternoon, Rachel let the group say anything they wanted to whoever was sharing. *That's bullshit. I think you're lying. Get honest. I can't believe this crap.* Rachel never smiled or showed affection. Neither did Russell Dean, the other counselor. Did they like her or hate her? Did they approve or disapprove? Did they think she was smart or stupid? And why did she care? Why did she always have to care so much about what everyone thought? Because it mattered, that's why. And it wasn't depression and it wasn't a disorder just because you wanted everyone to love you and wanted to make sure they did, because if everyone did love you and you knew it, wouldn't you be confident and happy for the rest of your life, no matter what? Wouldn't panic disappear? Wouldn't Myra be able to say what she wanted and learn what was important and understand everything? Wouldn't she be brave enough to be herself?

**

Why they didn't make out at One Tree Myra had no idea. She was waiting for him to lean over, to kiss her softly and open his mouth like Frisco Jones did with Felicia on *General Hospital*, the way all those fairy-tale forces of men pulled women close in fits of passion. Maybe Chad Norris would lean over and kiss her, feel for the snap of her jeans, reach under her pink Izod shirt. But this didn't happen. They drank. She thought for a moment of her heart, which the doctor said might stop beating if she drank alcohol. Because Myra was on Elavil, he had said.

Oh well.

"So when is your next game?" Myra asked.

"Friday." He didn't look at her, sipped his beer. Myra listened to all the moos and tried to guess where the cows were.

They left and drove to Chad's house. The doors were unlocked. His mom was out of town, he said. It was dark inside except for a light over the electric stove that illuminated a pot full of hardened ramen noodles, dried spills and crumbs on the counter, dishes layered in the sink, brown paneling on the walls. Chad opened the refrigerator and gave Myra a beer and gave himself one and then went to take a shower. Myra stood in the kitchen, buzzing hard. She drank the whole beer and then another one, afraid to move, because where should she go? He had given her a beer, so he wasn't expecting her to leave. Where should she put her empty can? She walked into the living room, moonlight shining in, and sat in the dark on a couch, listening for the shower to go off in the bathroom. She saw a television in one corner, dirty glasses on a coffee table, a desk with an electric typewriter, paper trash piled around. Should she turn on a light? From behind her ear, she pulled out some hair and circled the strands around her beer can until they were wet. Crickets chirped outside.

The shower stopped. Myra's heart pounded like drumbeats, her super-buzz turning to drunkenness, her vagina swelling. Thinking about him made her wet. She was a virgin, and at that moment she did not care about saving herself for that special night, that crystalline moment in time where apparently so much was lost.

She tried to keep from panting. She waited.

She heard Chad leave the bathroom, heard him moving around. Then nothing.

Was he coming back?

She finished her beer and walked into the hallway, where the door to his room was open and he lay in bed with his eyes closed. The bathroom light was on, shining through the open door, and Myra saw that Chad's sheets were printed with baseball gloves and balls and bats, like a bed set for a toddler. Myra smelled soap and saw that his hair was damp against his pillow. Myra couldn't tell if he was asleep or awake, but she knelt down by his bed, terrified, eager like a child. She could not stop herself.

"Chad?" she whispered, her head closer to his than it had ever been. She put her hand on his bare shoulder. His skin was warm.

He opened his eyes, gazed at her, and pulled her in, kissed her, opened his mouth. His kisses were amazing, soft and strong deep into her mouth, and she hoped she was following along well, that she was doing everything right, that he would like her breasts, still inside her bra, and he seemed to, he squeezed and squeezed and rubbed and she took off her shirt and then he was kissing her again, Chad Norris was kissing her and then he unsnapped her pants and pulled them down fast and climbed onto her and when he put his penis in, it hurt a little but not that much because she was so wet.

Now he would know everything. He would know how much she wanted him and how he could ask her to do anything anytime anywhere—now he knew all of that because the fluid that she had never known what to do with was staining his sheets, exposing it all. And she wished he did not know because as he thrust she knew that he did not love her, that he would have fallen asleep and forgotten about her out there in the dark if she had not come in, that he had never looked at or spoken to her with any interest, really, at all—that he was as indifferent to Myra as he was to the dirty dishes he was probably supposed to wash before his mom came back. He got up and left Myra sopping in his bed and lay down on the living room couch and fell immediately asleep.

Myra felt a stone of truth heavy in her gut, deep in her anatomy, somewhere in her body… her intestines, maybe? Weren't they actually hundreds of feet long?

Myra sat up, felt something lurch, and vomited hard, splattering the baseball sheets and the carpet. She took off his pillowcase, wiped her calves with them, stood up, put on her jeans and shirt, took beer from his refrigerator, and left. She drank one on her way down his creaky back stairs and threw the empty in his yard and got into the Nova. She was less drunk now—she felt a little sick and lightheaded but totally in control. She would go back and find that poor cat and take it home. Dead, alive, injured—she would take care of it.

She turned the key, but the Nova would not start.

***

She would never tell the Community about Chad Norris, but she was ready to share other meaningful things. Here, it was fine to tell everyone about what you were thinking and feeling and what had happened to you. Everybody did. One patient, Lisa with the straight bangs, drug of choice heroin, had run away from home to get away from a cousin who molested her. She lived by a freeway for six months, then overdosed, and someone had taken her to an emergency room. Bryan with the weird stubble, drug of choice rush, had tried every drug there was every day of his life since he was ten years old because his mother was always gone and her boyfriend beat him, and in high school he'd met a group of boys who dropped acid and smoked pot in a van before school. One morning they shared a fifth of bourbon, and Bryan had passed out in abnormal psychology class, slumped into his desk and then dropped onto the floor right in the front row. Theresa with the freckly arms, drug of choice pot, had snuck out of her home one night and gotten hit by a car while high on paint.

Myra would tell them what happened. But she wasn't about to tell them how Chad Norris had used her and cared nothing for her, and she especially wouldn't tell them how much she still adored him, loved him, desired him, would have let him inattentively fuck her all he wanted just to feel his touch and hear his voice and keep him near.

So she told them how she picked her friend up from baseball practice, that they were drinking beer at his house and he passed out, so she found a baseball bat by a garbage can and opened the hood of the Nova and banged the starter, then ran over to the ignition to try and get it to start. This method had never worked before—it always took two people, one banging on the starter and the other turning the key. She prayed again, turned the key. Silence. So she drank three beers as fast as she could, one after the other after the other, because one of the best feelings of her life was drinking a lot at once and then feeling herself get drunk after she wasn't drinking anymore. That invisible rush. She felt herself rise and wondered what she was going to do; she remembered, vaguely, walking down her friend's driveway, smoking and coughing and occasionally spitting if vomit rose in her throat. She remembered standing on the side of the road, eyes closed, feeling the drunk come on and breathing it in with bliss. She tripped and wobbled and swayed her way back to One Tree. The country night was empty.

She woke up on the slab. It was morning and a police officer was standing over her. She looked down at Myra through mirrored sunglasses and Myra saw herself in them, saw that her white face and brown hair with shiny barrettes in the officer's glasses looked warped and blurred and unlike Myra in every way—was that her, with her forearm up over her eyes?

"I'm Officer Jane. Your father is worried sick about you." She led Myra to the back of the police car, closed the door.

Myra became aware of her heart, the way it beat fast and heavy like a premonition. She put her hand on her chest and willed it to slow down. It didn't. Myra swallowed with what little saliva she could generate, looked out the window at the barbed wire fence line and then at the grey dirt smudges on the tops of her Tretorn shoes. Please please please, she asked God, in whom she only believed when she thought she might die, which was whenever she woke up after getting drunk. Please give me one more chance.

Jane pulled onto the road and spoke into the CB microphone she held in one hand. It occurred to Myra that if she died, Jane could revive her! Phew!

But she would not tell them about that, either. She shifted positions in her chair. This was stressful, deciding what to say as she said it. Not about the Elavil. Or why she got put on it or that when she started drinking she forgot about what the psychiatrist said, because getting drunk felt so good. She twirled the sash ends of her bathrobe around her fingers. For their first five days, so they would know how sick they were, patients had to wear hospital pajamas—tiny blue paisleys printed on white fabric, thin as used paper. After that, for the rest of their sixty-day stay, they could be in their own clothes.

"What time is it?" Myra asked.

"Six-fifteen a.m.," said Officer Jane. Minutes passed and her heart slowed and Myra was alive, the sun warming her face through the window and then shadowed by her house as Jane pulled into the alley. She was alive. She was not going to die. Her father Keen ran down the front steps and hugged his daughter, then pushed her away, held her out like a shirt.

"You've been drinking." He was a tower over her, tall and sturdy, brown faded bathrobe hanging only to his knees. The neighbor from across the alley walked onto her front porch, watching. Myra picked sleep out of her left eye.

"She's on medication," Keen said to Officer Jane, keeping his hands on Myra's shoulders. "She might die."

"I'll take you both to the hospital right now."

"No way!" said Myra.

"Let me get my wallet," said Keen.

"No! Dad!"

He put his hands on her shoulders and looked down at her and Myra felt a warmth in her spine, in the back of her neck. She forgot her headache and Chad Norris and how thirsty she was and felt just her father, paying attention to her—uplifting, true, divine.

"After that," Myra told them, "I had to wait to be admitted for seven days because you were full, but my dad forced me into the hospital so I wouldn't drink until I came here. Or kill myself or anything. Not that I would have. I guess my dad was just worried." Lie? Omission? Both? She had threatened to kill herself if her father sent her to rehab—she just hadn't been serious about it. But she couldn't tell them this, either, or that whenever she lied, she felt a twinge of guilt, shame, discomfort. It was always a betrayal.

"And I went ahead and got a tonsillectomy that I had needed for a long time anyway." She held up her paper cup of water.

"That's why I always have this, because my throat still hurts." She looked at all the patient faces, their expressions absorbed with her, the circle bright with their attention. The room was clean. The long tables on which they ate meals were folded up neatly and lined against the wall on the other side of the room. A technician named Bliss, who looked like the most bliss-less person Myra had ever seen, stood with her arms crossed in the wide doorframe that led to the hallway.

"That's it," Myra said. The windows were not textured like the ones in the patients' rooms, so Myra could see outside: giant hospital parking lot, busy street, gas stations, billboards, miniature urban strip in the distance that led to Interstate 235. "I'm done."

"Glad you're here, Myra," said Charlie with the yellow-blond hair, drug of choice LSD. He crossed his legs. Myra had never seen a boy cross his legs before. Not Chad Norris, not Mark, not any boy she had ever known.

"Glad you're here," said Stephanie with the blue mascara, drug of choice alcohol.

"Welcome," said Jen with the short legs, drug of choice pot.

"I'm *so* glad you're here," said Billy with the white-blond hair, drug of choice whatever the hell. His nose was upturned, his face narrow. "Wow."

Bliss the tech stared at her—no smile, no frown. Myra wanted Bliss to love her and wanted all of them to love her and thought they might already. She clasped her hands together to keep from pulling out her hair.

Baby Birds

Myra loved plaster walls. Elongated torsos, distorted farm animals, puffs almost like clouds. Myra sat in one of the study carrels built into two walls of the common room where they all ate meals and had Community—but instead of doing the homework that her teachers had assembled and mailed to her, she ran the fleshiest part of her pinky over and over a barbed animal tail. Or maybe it was the tip of a crown on a faceless, misshapen head, or the beak of a baby bird, the way its wing reached up for a mother. Melanie had died in a car accident when Myra was five and Myra remembered her all the time, with big hands like her father's and wiry, coarse hair.

It was hard for Myra to believe that an artist crafted none of these images that looked so deliberate—but surely they had been brushed onto the wall and left to dry into whatever they became.

A hand dropped a note on the edge of her desktop. Lined paper folded up tight.

"Read it later," Charlie with the yellow-blond hair, drug of choice LSD, whispered to her. She felt his body tall behind her, recognized his voice. She wanted to run underneath something, hide herself. She didn't dare turn around.

Charlie had barely spoken to her since the day she arrived, since she had refused to give Keen a hug goodbye at the front desk, since Grace the nurse took her on the elevator up to the two floors of the treatment unit and took her suitcase.

"That's my stuff," said Myra.

"We're searching it for drugs and alcohol."

"That suitcase was my mom's." Yellow with brown leather stripes down each side, the surface like thick cardboard and full of scratches.

"You'll get it back."

"My Winnie the Pooh is in there." Old. It crackled when you squeezed it.

"You'll get that back, too."

Grace walked her to her room and told her to change into the requisite pajamas—because she was sick, that's why—and then took her into the Community while the patients were on after-dinner Smoke Break. Myra had pulled her Camels from the pocket of her robe and lit one with the lighter provided on the table, a long table with plastic coating over plasticized wood. Twelve kids sat around it in metal folding chairs, talking over an industrial fan housed in metal and mounted into one corner of the ceiling.

Billy with the platinum hair, drug of choice whatever the hell, had been the first one to approach her. "Hey." He sat down, flicked his Marlboro into the black plastic ashtray. He placed two other cigarettes before him and spaced them evenly apart.

"Hi."

"So how did you get here?"

"My dad put me in," she said.

"It's his fault, huh?"

She puffed.

"I'm Billy."

"I'm Myra."

"I'm glad you're here."

She put out her cigarette.

"You should light another one. There's time for three if you hurry."

Two in a row dried out her throat and hurt her stitches.

"Okay," she said, lighting a second one. The other kids were singing "Hotel California," tapping their hands on the table. Charlie pulled up a chair next to them. "I got reamed today, Billy." His hair hung to the middle of his back, his nose doughy. He was cute in a not very cute way.

"What did you do?" Myra asked.

"Had sex last weekend when I was home." He looked right at Myra when he spoke. No shame, no hesitation.

"Charlie's on a No Sex Contract," Billy said.

"Now for a whole year." Charlie sighed. "That's going to be hard."

Myra was not a virgin. She wanted to tell them that. She wanted to tell everyone everything all the time and had to stop herself so often that it made her lonesome even when she was happy. Which made no sense at all.

"I'm Charlie," he had said, holding out his hand. Myra shook it and felt her wrist drooping like a pretend queen. She blushed.

Myra put Charlie's note in her pocket—the pocket of her jeans, now that she was on Day Seven and out of pajamas. She looked over her shoulder. The common room was empty except for the folded tables and chairs against the far wall and the rest of the patients who were Myra's age, high school juniors, about six of them altogether, sitting in the carrels. Jen with the bright red hair, drug of choice pot, looked up from her work and smiled at Myra. Jen had attached herself to Myra like the invisible mother bird in the plaster, educating her, assuring Myra that she was indeed chemically dependent and sick, that she was where she needed to be. And Myra did feel better now—those pajamas had made her feel unkempt and slothful, even though she had showered every morning and feathered her hair with her curling iron and brushed it into place with her vent brush and covered her patches—an under-layer of them now—with barrettes and bobby pins and sprayed it all stiff with Aqua Net Extra Hold. Jen used Aqua Net, too, but sprayed it when her hair was still wet, then brushed the sides back and secured them with sparkling sliver barrettes so that her head looked helmeted in slick, metallic orange, her bangs curled into place like a waxed mustache. Jen was working her Twelve Step program all the time. She talked to techs one-on-one about pages in the *Alcoholics Anonymous Big Book*, which treatment at OPP was based on.

"All rehabs are," Jen explained. "Bliss said so. That's how much it works." Jen confronted girls in Small Group and everyone in Community with their transgressions. She shared and cried a lot, exposing herself to all of them. She seemed overcome by energy and momentum with God and faith and hope for herself, which many of them did not have.

On Myra's Day Three, Jen had told Myra her story. They had been sitting in the lounge—a room just off the common room that reminded Myra of an observation car on an Amtrak, with bay windows overlooking the Des Moines River and the lawn sloping toward it, sidewalk striping though the green and thinning into manicured banks. The horizon line beyond was lined with structures and buildings, the sun smoky yellow and fading. The constant sky. Myra knew nothing about Des Moines, the capital of her state. She knew nothing about Iowa except that there were lots of farmers, lots of cornfields, dots of small towns along Interstate 80. If you took Highway 6 instead, you drove right through them and they looked vacant and bereft and Myra did not know why. She had been born in Iowa City, an unabandoned place of activity and restaurants and a city park, Iowa River running through the middle. The University of Iowa art museum had exhibits from all over the world—her mother had worked there. Images of her were always moving through: her back to Myra as she stood at the stove in a long nightgown; her hands resting on her lap and Myra playing with them, squishing the blue line of vein into the skin-surface of bone; her voice loud from upstairs as she yelled for Keen while Myra sat on the bottom stair. Myra remembered the memorial service, which had been at the public library because her family did not believe in God. Keen despised religion.

"So did your mother," he said as he drove them home after the service, the Nova clean and unbroken.

"If you apply the basic tenets of logic to any of it," he said. "The whole thing falls apart. It's like a building with no structure."

Why wasn't her father crying? Why wasn't she?

All the patients at Our Primary Purpose eventually believed in God, like Jen. Jen said you had to if you wanted to be sober, and she was always looking for His will. She said her whole story had been about her doing what she wanted, not what God wanted. She had started with pot, smoked it all day every day for two years—joints with her boyfriend after shop class in the back of the high school in Mason City, where she was from, and before that with her brother in the alley behind their apartment. This year, after her boyfriend dumped her, she'd gone from all Bs to all Fs and chugged Absolut from her friend's mother's freezer.

These stories had become to Myra like superficial parts of sentences, like non-restrictive clauses; she didn't need to understand anything. They rained from patients' mouths in showers, quick torrents every day.

"I almost died," Jen continued. "I woke up in a hospital."

"What if they tell me I'm not chemically dependent?" Myra asked. Rachel would tell her soon whether she was.

Jen raised her eyebrows at Myra and looked amused by the question, almost like a counselor. Jen was thin and tiny. Her feet almost didn't reach the floor. "Just about everyone here is chemically dependent. I mean, how would you have gotten here if you weren't?"

"What if it was just the situation I was in?"

"Then they'll tell you that you're not, and they'll send you home. But that hardly ever happens."

Jen stared at Myra so hard that Myra turned away.

"And you definitely seem chemically dependent to me."

"Can't they be wrong?"

"Nope. They know what they're doing. They study you. They talk to your family. They meet all together and then diagnose you."

Myra felt something inside her deflate. Her shoulders relaxed and she hadn't even realized they were stiff. She looked at Jen curiously.

"You can trust them," Jen said.

So Myra was a center of their attention. Rachel, Bliss the tech, Grace the nurse, Russell Dean, and the others whose names she didn't know yet—the nurse who brought her Elavil every night, the skinny, pretty counselor with hair like Farah Fawcett who led them in Recreation and group exercise—they all talked about Myra. They wrote notes in her chart for one another to read about what she said, how she said it, what she asked for, what she ate, who she talked to, what she said she felt. Most of the counselors and techs were recovering addicts themselves, Jen reminded Myra.

"Really, you can trust them. I swear."

Myra felt like she was in a crib, surrounded by nurture, tiny and attended to. They were experts. Professionals. And they were more focused on her than anyone had ever been. Of course she could trust them.

So Myra had woken up the next morning more content than she had felt in months, years, ever. She happily gave away her single-serve box of Frosted Flakes and didn't complain about the eggs. She didn't pull out her hair when she went to the bathroom or when no one was looking. During morning Small Group she tried to listen to Rachel despite the fact that Myra did not like her— her stiff mouth, her hair curled tight into her head, the way she looked at Myra and every girl as if she were lying no matter what. But Myra listened anyway. She tried to present herself with a new aura of openness, and when Small Group was over and they stood to make a circle, Myra held their hands and said the Serenity Prayer and tried to feel the words in her heart. She told herself that serenity was an answer. She ate her lunch with Jen, and she tried to listen to all that Jen said.

But now Charlie's note was in her pocket. She forgot Easy Does It and Let Go and Let God and First Things First and the rush of peace she felt when she prayed. She got up and felt his warm square against her hip and asked Bliss if she could go to the bathroom.

The night before, during Community, Charlie had said he was hoping his primary counselor Russell Dean would let him attend his high school graduation, two weeks away. He sat in the circle with his hands clasped and his elbows on his knees, his hair covering his face until he tucked it behind his ears.

"I'm on day thirty-four," he said. "And it's okay with my mom and dad. They'll pick me up and bring me right back. No parties, no nothing. I'm not going to use, and I won't have sex like I did before! I know I fucked up! I swear I'll run if they don't let me go." Russell Dean had said they would have to wait and see; as the day grew nearer, he would discuss it in one of the staff meetings and the counselors and techs would make a decision together. For now, Russell Dean said, Charlie needed to live in the moment.

"Let it go, man," Billy said. "Work your program."

"But it's my graduation," he lamented. When he was done, he sat back in his seat and crossed his legs. It was such an effeminate position, yet Charlie seemed so comfortable taking it, with his hair, with himself.

Myra walked into a stall and flushed the toilet to drown out any crinkle of the paper while she opened the note. Bliss would hear it. Bliss could hear anything.

A drawing in pencil of a girl from the waist up. A girl that was meant to be Myra, except Myra had a shorter neck and smaller breasts and a rounder face. Myra's eyes weren't that big either. But he had drawn Myra's hair and renditions of her barrettes and clips in a way that made her look fashionable, different, unique. Did she really look that cool? The neck of her T-shirt was ridged, the background of the sketch shaded and shadowed, especially around her shoulders and face, to give her shape, substance.

Myra realized she was sweating. She sat down on the toilet seat. In the lower right corner were the tiniest words, written in cursive: "Myra—I love drawing you. Charlie."

Myra gazed at Charlie's vision of her, this self she had never seen before. Tingles pierced her cheeks, the sides of her neck. She attempted to swallow.

Normalcy

Charlie's house was large, three stories, in a Des Moines suburb with a lush, green lawn that no one in his family took care of. That was for the lawn guys, who came once a week to mow and rake and manicure while Charlie tripped in his room and smoked joints and blew evidence out the window, which he kept doing even after his mother caught him. As if his mother would ignore it this time and continue reading the newspaper, as if his father would overlook it this time and continue eating his veal cutlet. Charlie kept trying to hide it, getting caught, trying to hide it, getting caught. A steady drum.

"That's a cry for help," Russell Dean said. "We all did it. We all do it."

But Charlie hadn't wanted help, just to get high in his own space, in his own room with its soft carpet and drafting table and bed with giant cushions and dark, sparkling rock posters on the walls. His parents would only ground him, which gave him more time in his room to trip. Couldn't smell that, could they? He started to climb out his window and sit on the roof to smoke, to study the slopes of other housetops so much like his: pale streets winding into a plain of golf course. He brought his sketchpad and drew the neighborhood.

But they still smelled it. His father had even caught him out there once with a joint in his hand, grinning like a joker, his boom box playing Iron Maiden.

And yet he still did it.

"You embody the definition of insanity," Russell Dean said.

"Doing the same thing over and over again and expecting different results," said Billy.

But it was the acid that got him sent to treatment. The baggie with five squares that he'd left in his pocket was found by the housekeeper.

"Is this drugs?" His mother asked, shaking the baggie, holding it out his window as he sat on the roof. "Is it?"

His mother was home that Saturday, but Charlie had taken a hit anyway. They had never been able to tell; his parents had never done drugs in their lives. Always heading upward. Driven and focused. High-powered Iowans.

Did they even know what acid was? They didn't know what they were missing. Maybe they should try it!

Had he just yelled this at his mother? He wasn't sure. Shit. He felt vibrations move in his throat and realized he had definitely used his voice. He stared at the speckle of shingle imprints in his palm and felt them with his index finger as if he were reading his fortune. He closed his eyes and felt the texture soak up his arm and into his neck and into his mind. The bumps took over.

"LSD?"

He kept his eyes closed and rubbed his palm on the tip of his nose.

"Come inside immediately," she said, crying now. "Be careful," she said. "Oh God. Take my hand."

He scooted over on his butt, took it. Cold fingers. "I'm calling your father home from work."

When he climbed inside, she stood at the open window and held him. He closed his eyes as she stroked his hair and said My Charlie over and over, like a lullaby.

Peaking With Parents, he thought. Or—Peaking in the Company of Parents. A painting bright with tragedy.

Spins

In sixth grade, Myra and her friend had shared a can of beer. She hadn't even gotten drunk.

"So you were drinking in sixth grade?" asked Lisa with the straight bangs, drug of choice heroin. She was only fourteen.

"We stole it from their fridge," Myra said. She was the focus of Small Group that morning to give her Tell-All. This was what every patient did on Day Nine.

"Why didn't you drink more?" asked Theresa with the freckly arms, drug of choice pot. Theresa was a tough girl from Mount Pleasant. She wore Foghat and Lynyrd Skynyrd T-shirts—inside out, since music shirts weren't allowed—and had a wide smile. She was seventeen, she'd been in rehab twice before, and if she didn't stay sober this time they'd put her in a lock-up.

"I don't remember."

"Oh, bull*shit*. You didn't drink more your first time trying beer?"

"I don't think so."

"You're lying," said Theresa. "Takes a liar to know one, and I know you're lying."

"I'm not lying." Myra looked at Rachel, who said nothing as usual, her gaze centered on the middle of their circle as Myra spoke. Behind Rachel was her desk and a wall with two windows that looked into the building next door—another part of the hospital. The blinds in that building were always shut.

Myra wasn't lying. What else could she say?

"Maybe her mom came in and caught us? Maybe that's why we stopped."

"Uh-huh."

"We thought it tasted like gross water or something."

"But you kept drinking until you were caught?"

"We didn't get caught."

"So you chose to stop?" Rachel finally said something.

"I guess so."

The second time was in eighth grade. Orange wine coolers with a handful of friends. They stuffed some bottles into their jackets and walked to the Sycamore Mall to see the movie *Night of the Comet*, and yes, Myra had been drunk. They sat in the very back row. Halfway through, when Kelli Maroney was in the department store, dancing to "Living on the Edge," and trying on all the clothes she had ever wanted because everyone else in the world had died, Myra dropped an empty bottle on the floor. It clinked loud against the cement and rolled down to the middle of the theater, and they were all covering their mouths, laughing and laughing and trying to be quiet. Myra was terrified of getting caught and kicked out, but the terror was almost amusing, more intangible than terror had ever felt because her drunkenness kept the terror at a distance, at the edge of haze and uplift—but still Myra was aware of her skin, the sweat that began to spread, the undercurrent of worry, and she pulled on her friend Cindy's arm and made her leave. They walked back home and got headaches and Cindy puked and went to sleep.

"What about drugs?"

"I haven't done any."

"Bullshit," said Theresa.

"I haven't. Ever."

"Rachel, isn't your bullshit radar going off?"

"Russell Dean is the one with the bullshit radar," said Rachel. She nodded at Myra. "Continue."

"Well, we know when people are lying," said Theresa. She pointed to Rachel. "Especially them. They always know."

"I'm not lying."

And she wasn't, and since Rachel seemed to know she wasn't, Myra did not understand why she didn't tell Theresa to let her finish.

The first time Myra got in trouble for drinking—the night everything changed—was the night she first hung out with Nancy. It was the summer before Myra's junior year. She had been at a party in someone's driveway, a high school party with boys and girls standing around by a keg and more kids arriving every second, filling up space in the carport. Myra arrived with Cindy—still her friend then—but Cindy had gone inside to find the bathroom, and that's when Nancy had come up to Myra.

"Drink beer with me." Nancy always wore her black leather jacket and tight Levi's and black boots, her short hair dyed to match. She did drugs and she was a dropout, according to everyone, but Myra often saw her in the hallways, her tiny purse atop the stack of books she held against her chest. They had had a conversation once, in the girls' room on the second floor of City High, and Nancy had offered Myra her lip gloss.

Nancy grabbed Myra's hand and pulled her toward the keg, and Myra realized that she would follow Nancy anywhere. She was so cool and easy and confident, with such clear skin and a perfect chin and a smooth voice.

"Cooper and me broke up." Nancy grabbed a cup and filled it, handed it to Myra, and got one for herself.

"You did?" Led Zeppelin boomed from inside the house. Boys sitting on the stairs leading into the kitchen were smoking cigarettes.

"Want one?" said Nancy. She held one out. Myra had never smoked a cigarette and had never wanted to. She took it. "He cheated on me."

"No way!" said Myra. Everyone knew Cooper—Nancy's boyfriend—already graduated. He dropped her off at City High every morning in the parking lot by the auditorium and then waited there at the end of the day to pick her up, motorcycle engine running.

"Trinity Taylor. Slut," Nancy said, lighting her cigarette. She reached over to light Myra's but someone bumped into her and Myra dropped it.

"Here, Sweetie." Nancy pulled the cigarette from her own mouth and handed it to Myra. "I've got plenty."

It got packed and loud and there were eighth graders running around in the backyard and a black dog on a chain barking and barking. Myra might have had two beers and she was drinking a third when—

"Two beers? That's it?" said Theresa.

"Now I don't believe you either," said Jen. "You're minimizing."

"Yep," said Tina with the off-center eyes, drug of choice cocaine. Her neighbor had raped her for three years, from age seven to ten. She was on Day Forty-five and didn't speak often and had large spaces between her teeth.

"I had two, I think. I don't remember."

"Then you had a lot more than that."

"It was almost a year ago. I don't remember." Did she? Maybe it was more than two after all. She was drunk by then, a little bit, just enough to see everything around her as warmth. As welcoming. Then they heard the motorcycle.

"That asshole!" Nancy yelled. "I can't believe he came here!" She grabbed Myra's hand and pulled her through the backyard and into the woodsy end of the cul-de-sac, Myra following her through the trees that she could not name and then into the street on the other side of the block. They started walking, Nancy's boots clicking on the concrete and her hair frizzing beneath the streetlamps, Myra's Kmart shoes padding quietly alongside. Next to Nancy, Myra saw herself: hair straight and feathered stiff on the sides, white skin with ruddy cheeks, green and pink and white plaid shirt, jean shorts, woven loop belt. She felt minuscule, underrepresented, styleless, and without form. Did Nancy think of Myra as a friend? She felt flattered and tried to fight it, to talk herself out of feeling flattered by the attention of someone she found interesting or gorgeous or smart or lovely, because if she ever felt too secure in love and attention they would turn to nothingness before she even knew they were gone, like stars disappearing as night turned to day. Myra showed Nancy where the North Star was but Myra did know that—Keen had shown her one night in their backyard. She remembered because whenever Keen did share parts of his life or knowledge, those moments in time were precious, remarkable. They left Myra so badly wanting more that she found herself playing the scenes over and over.

They stopped and sat on the curb. Nancy stuck her feet into the street and crossed her legs, toes of her boots pointing to the sky. The houses all around them were void of lights and sound, the streets scrubbed clean, fireflies blinking above mowed lawns.

"I'm tired," said Nancy.

Myra sat down and hugged her knees, resting her chin in the dip between them.

As if from God came a Trans Am from around the corner, a pair of thick white stripes down each side. Two boys got out.

"Dave! Oh my god, Dave!" Nancy jumped up and hugged him. He hugged her back. Myra knew Dave because everyone did—a thick, cute, champion wrestler who had just graduated. He'd been Homecoming King. The other one was Mark, a senior, a football player with blue eyes and a slight under bite. They were both tall, really tall, and popular and cute and Myra wanted to cover herself. Why was she so afraid? She had always been afraid, even though her head was full of conversations she wanted to have and images of the way she wanted to present herself, to appear, to seem to other people. And what was she afraid *of*? She'd understood it when Judy, the counselor she'd seen when she was fourteen, had told her she was afraid of rejection and abandonment because her mother had died. But Myra also understood how illogical this fear was when Judy tried to make her fear go away. *So what if someone doesn't like you?* she asked. *What does it mean if someone doesn't like you?* And Myra offered answers that were stupid, that made no sense when you said them out loud or wrote them down. *That I am unlikable. That I am ugly. That I am alone and no one will be my friend. That I will never know love or be loved.* She knew those answers were not true, that when you saw them written on paper or said them out loud, you could see how wrong they were. Myra knew her views were distorted.

But still, they did not go away.

Myra told Small Group none of her reflections. And they weren't asking why about much of anything other than what she did and whether she drank or not.

Nancy put her head on Dave's shoulder. "He fucking cheated, Dave." She put her arms around his neck. "He cheated."

"I know, I know. He's sorry, though. He's looking for you."

"I'm Mark," Mark said to Myra.

"Hi. I'm Myra." She pretended to be confident, as if boys like Mark said hi to her every day. As if they were blips.

"I know," he said smiling, that tiny under bite disappearing into his dimples. "Want a beer? We have some in the backseat."

"You know?" asked Myra, still looking at Mark who was still looking at her.

"I've seen you around."

Something in Myra's belly fluttered like a bird. She thought it might be her entire stomach, but she didn't know how large stomachs were, or even where they were—wasn't the stomach higher up the body, closer to the heart than the hips? This anatomy would make sense since Myra felt what she thought was a tornado in her stomach, swirling inside, her anticipation so intense that it made her gasp and then laugh. She smiled and felt the power of it for the first time. Mark gazed at her. Myra gazed back, stunned by her own confidence.

Her curfew was midnight.

"Call your mom," said Nancy.

"You mean my dad," said Myra.

"Let's go to the pay phone at 7-Eleven so Myra can call her mom and say she's staying at my house." Nancy was sitting in the back seat with Dave; they wanted to go to Court Hill Park, a few blocks away.

"How many beers had you drank?" asked Jen.

"Two, I think," Myra said.

"What a minimizer!" said Theresa. She crossed her arms like Rachel.

"I really don't remember," said Myra. Did she? She remembered standing under the light above the pay phone outside of the 7-Eleven, the parking lot empty, the streets quiet. Nancy stood beside her, telling her what to say, and Myra kept telling Nancy to shh. She remembered her father asking questions in a sleepy voice and being aware that her call had woken him up, and she remembered getting annoyed that he wouldn't let her off the phone because Mark was waiting in the car and she had to go with them tonight because there would never be another moment in time like this one, one where she could be with Mark and see if he actually liked her. She would not let this opportunity disappear. And why did these moments of potential security and love and desire always have to be moments, flickers? Why couldn't a moment last longer than a minute? Why not hours, days? Why couldn't her life be full of security and contentment all the time? What was so wrong with a desire for such an existence?

Myra sighed hard into the receiver, waved her hand in front of her nose to disperse the gnats and told her father she would see him in the morning. Then she hung up. Her father might have been finished talking. He might have said fine. He might have been in the middle of another question. Myra had no idea.

"If she's home, my mom will cover for you," said Nancy. "Let's go!"

Mark drove them all to Court Hill. They got the beer out of the car. Myra and Mark took the shelter by the weeping willow and Nancy and Dave took the shelter across the footbridge, on the other side of the creek that Myra did not know the name of. Myra and Mark kissed on the bench for hours, mouths opening and closing. His lips were soft like the moonlight. He told her she was pretty, that she had a beautiful smile. He stroked her hair. He reached up her shirt and she let him—she had never felt anyone's hands on her breasts—they were so white, full, never exposed to sun or elements or anything in the outside world—and the light above the shelter was out and it was just dark enough for them to keep from seeing one another clearly. Everything was new. The palms of his hands on her nipples and the gentle pressure of his fingers when he squeezed made her feel soft, sweet, beautiful. Grown-up. She felt sexual and sensual but didn't know those words, what they meant if they emerged from inside you without the timbre of vocabulary, the shape of meaning.

Between long stretches of making out, they talked about school starting soon, about how much he loved football (he was on varsity, first string), how maybe they could have a great rest-of-summer together before his practices started.

"What are you doing over there?" Dave called. Nancy laughed.

Mark didn't answer. He pulled Myra gently against his chest and wrapped his arm around her. He rubbed one of her shoulders.

Myra became aware that she could see the weeping willow, that the night had begun to fade, that this extensive string of moments was ending. When Dave and Nancy walked over, no one knew what time it was. The shingled rooftops of one-story homes all around them were visible against the gray sky. No breeze blew. The neighborhood was as quiet and still as it had been the night before, when Mark and Dave found them on the curb.

Myra had never been so thirsty, and she had to get home before her father woke up, and if he was awake, he couldn't possibly see Myra being dropped off by two boys.

Nancy asked Myra if she had any money for a taxi.

"Because they can take me home," Nancy said. "My mom won't care. I bet yours will."

"Could you take me close to my house?" Myra said. They were getting into Mark's Trans Am.

Dave leaned down to the open window on the driver's side to Mark, who was starting the car. "I'll walk, man." He looked back at Nancy. "Call Cooper. I'll bet he's worried about you."

"Huh! No way." She put her feet up on the seat and looked out the window.

"I'll bet he's waiting for you at your house."

"Who cares?" Nancy did not look at any of them. The pink shirt beneath her leather jacket had a spot of beer just below the collar.

Mark drove Nancy to her house—a duplex out by the Sycamore Mall, a duplex with no cars in the driveway and nothing in the front yard except a German Shepherd on a chain and a doghouse. The dog did not move or open its eyes, as if it were drugged, exhausted, ill, indifferent. Myra got out of the front seat and flipped it forward for Nancy. No large trees out here. The sun was blinding.

"Bye," said Myra. Why wasn't Nancy talking? Even looking at her anymore?

"Bye," Nancy said. She bent down and petted the dog. "Hey, Butch, sweetie. Hey there." She sat on the concrete stoop.

On their way to Myra's house, Mark held her hand and Myra sat between the seats, right next to him, their hips touching. Mark asked if he could call her. She said yes. He dropped her off and kissed her goodbye in front of Black's Gaslight Village, a sprawling series of basement and first-floor apartments blocked from view by vines and trees that Myra knew were older than she was because they were all so thick and tall and old. Myra stood before the foliage and watched him drive away, started walking the half-block to her house.

"So how much did you drink that night, Myra?" Rachel asked.

"I don't know."

All the girls stared at her. Theresa rolled her eyes. So did Stephanie with the blue mascara, drug of choice alcohol.

"Maybe six?" Myra said.

"Six beers." Rachel nodded and leaned forward. Her front teeth were yellowish. "Do you know how much that is?"

Myra shook her head.

"How many times have you been drunk in your life?"

"I don't know."

"Weekends mostly?"

Myra nodded. Rachel had perfect fingernails. Pale pink polish, filed to dull squares instead of round tips.

"Both nights?"

"Not really. Sometimes."

"How many times when you were on Elavil?"

Myra scratched dried Aqua Net from one of her barrettes, a slender brown metal strip above her left ear. Shrugged. Felt her face turn angry.

"She asked you a question," said Tina.

"I don't know."

"I bet you don't," said Rachel. The two lights on the desk phone blinked red, little bubbles below the squares of buttons.

"If you're being honest," Rachel said. "That's easily over sixty times that you've been drunk."

Myra stared at her shoes, picked at her barrette again. Tina crossed her legs.

"Do you know how many times I've been drunk, Myra?"

Myra shook her head.

"I'm not chemically dependent," Rachel said. "I'm one of the only counselors here who isn't. I am a food addict and a co-dependent, but I've never been interested in alcohol. I'm a social drinker, a moderate drinker, a normal drinker."

Myra sat.

"I've been drunk five times. In my entire life. And once I realized I was drunk, I stopped. Every time. This is what social drinkers do. Do you think you're a normal, social drinker?"

Myra's legs and head hurt like they had that morning as she headed toward her house, but what had ached the most were her cheeks from smiling all night long. She'd never felt physical pain from elation before. She opened and closed her mouth, rubbed the flat fleshy places below her earlobes where her upper and lower jaws came together. What was she rubbing? Muscle? Ligament? Bone? She turned her head to stretch her neck and saw Millicent, their neighbor across the alley, sitting on her front porch. Staring strangely at Myra.

Myra waved.

"Have you called home?" Millicent asked.

In Old Iowa City, where Myra lived, there were miles of alleys that cut through square blocks from the Oakland Cemetery all the way to Dubuque Street, where fraternity houses the size of mansions lined the sloped banks of the Iowa River, white Greek letters cemented large into their lawns. Myra knew her alleys, which ones were pavement and which ones were gravel, what all the backyards looked like. Gardens, chicken wire fences, doghouses, overgrown lawns. Lots of the houses stretched toward the alley and revealed side door windows to a basement that was old and dirty with a cement floor, or modernized and carpeted with a twenty-six-inch color television, or renovated and rented out by graduate students. There were very few fences to shut people out. You could see everything. Myra felt certain that her knowledge was an advantage, but she didn't know why.

"Your dad's been looking for you." Millicent glared, and Myra saw herself standing on the sidewalk, recently felt up, clothes askew and hair matted out of its sprayed hold, and her legs smudged with dirt in a few places and pocked with mosquito bites.

"You might want to give him a call." Millicent went inside her house and slammed her front door.

"Myra!" Her father was running to her, wearing the brown bathrobe and slippers he had worn all of Myra's life. He was a big man, and when he wore his robe, his arms looked huge. He held them out in the morning light and before Myra could move they were around her, not letting her go. Myra wanted to run, to go back to Mark, back to the park and the softness. Her father smelled like cigarettes and sweat. He pushed her away and held her by her shoulders and looked at her. His baldness had progressed nearly to his ears, the dark gray hair that grew from the back of his head hanging loose, the gel he always combed in no longer holding. His skin wrinkled like leather around his eyes, large and blue—so different from Myra's. Thin glasses slipped down his nose as he spoke.

The street seemed endless behind him, stretching down into the city. "I've been up all night. I called the police."

"So you lied to him," said Jen.

Myra nodded.

"Where were you?" He yelled this time, furious. His eyes glistened with exhaustion. But he still wasn't letting her go. He kept his hands on her shoulders as if they were nailed in place.

"Do you know what that did to your dad?" asked Rachel. "Myra, have you thought about what that did to your dad?"

Myra shook her head.

"Have you thought about what your behavior and your choices have done to your father, Myra?"

He doesn't care, Myra didn't say. I'm not even on his radar. Myra opened her mouth to speak and became aware that she could not.

Rachel held up her palms. "Time for Myra to have a think. For the next three minutes, Myra is going to think about what her behavior might have done to her father. So nobody speak, please." She looked at Myra. "Picture him. That morning. Or the morning the cop brought you home from the country. Or the night you tried to kill yourself. Or any number of nights I'm sure you haven't told us anything about."

Myra bit her lip and reached up to scrape off more Aqua Net.

Rachel held up her palm again. "Do not touch your hair. Keep your hands away from it. Don't ever let me see you touch your hair. Sit there and leave your hands in your lap. Do not move."

Myra would not cry. She would bite a hole in her lip before she would let herself. Then she felt a tear on her cheek. Then another.

"Let them drip. You don't get to wipe them away."

Myra sniffled. She felt like the architect of everything built wrong, one structure after another, beams collapsing and deteriorating beneath her, over her head, all the way out into an invisible distant place in the earth.

Pledge

Her mother said Theresa looked like she was running a fever with all the blush on her cheeks.

"And you did the foundation wrong," she said, putting a plate of scrambled eggs in front of her.

"I don't care," said Theresa. She could smell the alcohol on her mother from the night before, as if a door had opened and let in a draft. Gross.

"You can still see your freckles. They're pitter-pattered underneath."

"Leave me alone." She ripped the crust off her toast and noticed where her cut had seeped into her shirt, a wet spot on the back of her wrist that covered a cut she'd made with her thumbnail the night before, after she got home from her shift at Wendy's. She managed the salad bar, rotated the food in the tan crocks so that the bottom of the crock was never visible. When the broccoli or hard-boiled eggs that smelled like formaldehyde or stale croutons ran out because Theresa couldn't keep up, Connie the manager yelled at her. Especially when the ice was low, which was the worst because Theresa had to fill a bucket, carry it into the dining room, scoop ice into her hands, and shape it around the crocks, her fingers growing numb. She often had to wipe ranch and French dressing and cottage cheese off the kale leaves, which were tucked around each crock to make the food look fresh and appetizing.

"Can you eat it?" she asked Connie once during training.

"No one eats kale," she said, laughing. Her short hair was dyed light brown and stuck straight out from the sides of her cap. "It's only for decoration."

Connie trained Theresa on the line, too, and busted her for spreading condiments incorrectly. "End to end!" she yelled. Theresa held the top half of a bun in one hand and a sandwich spreader in the other. They were in the middle of the dinner rush and the drive-through microphone wasn't working properly. The deep fryer beeped like a forklift, and the line of people stretched out the door.

"Huh?" Theresa asked.

Connie snatched the bun and spread the mayo around so it reached the edges of the circle. "You don't just plop it in the middle. Do it right and move faster."

"No one's going to complain about that," Theresa said.

"I'm not your mother. Don't mouth off to me."

But the money was worth it. She stared at her first paycheck as she walked home from work, held it in both her hands and stared at it and almost tripped on the sidewalk. $82.23. Four months later, she had saved almost all of it and picked up more hours. Connie bought them beers after work now and they drank them and smoked pot on the balcony of her apartment. Connie had her own place. A new stereo system. She sipped from her can of Coors and put the roach in a clip, blue feathers wisping in the air as she passed it to Theresa.

Connie had her own car, too. An old Ford Pinto with a tape deck. She wouldn't let anybody smoke in it, not even her boyfriend.

"He's used to it," she said. "He pretty much does whatever I say."

That's how Theresa wanted to be whenever she would have a boyfriend. She never wanted to put up with the shit her mother drank away. Theresa would never be like her. Never. She inhaled, burned her lip, opened another beer.

Truthfulness

Myra's father was sitting across the conference table—no plastic coating this time but a real wood oval with layers of varnished grain and a beveled edge. Was it mahogany? Myra knew that mahogany was a dark shade. Through the windows behind Rachel, a plain of graveled tar rooftop glinted in the sun. Beside her father was Russell Dean. Myra didn't know why he was here—she had never had group with him, he wasn't her counselor—but Myra never asked about things like this, about decisions they made, grateful to be so consistently a center of their attention. So she might have felt uncomfortable. So what? They knew what they were doing—she was becoming more accepting of this with the passing of each group, each session, each meal, each minute she spent at Our Primary Purpose. And Russell Dean was Charlie's counselor, so Myra felt Charlie here, too, watching her, as if he were privy to her secrets.

Her father was listening to her without responding, as Rachel had instructed. This meeting was Own Up, where patients told their families about every drug they had ever consumed and everything they had ever lied about. Patients got peer support during Own Up and Jen had volunteered—she sat next to Myra, listening and watching. The only thing missing was Myra's paper cup of water: Grace the nurse no longer let her have one to sip.

"You've been here fourteen days," she'd said. "Your tonsils should be healed up."

"My throat still hurts."

"Tough."

What was so terrible about her carrying water around? What if all of them carried cups of water around just because they wanted to? And Myra's throat really did hurt. Still. Every single time she swallowed. Her stitches might have melted away by now, but those tissues were raw and sore, vulnerable to saliva, to inhalations of smoke and air, to scratchy mouthfuls of the Lay's potato chips patients got sometimes with lunch—one of those tiny bags they sold at 7-Elevens for twenty-five cents—or crumbly crusts of toast they got with breakfast. Grace wanted to enforce her will, but all Myra wanted was cold water. It soothed the gape of skin in her pharynx where her tonsils used to be.

Myra stopped talking and looked at Rachel.

"Could I please have some water?"

"After Own Up," Rachel said. Myra had been so nervous beforehand that she trembled. It's okay, Rachel had said during their brief meeting that morning. Everyone is anxious before Own Up. Some patients even vomit. But they all felt better afterward, like a weight was removed.

"It brings most of you a lot of relief," said Rachel.

"That makes sense," said Myra.

"Any other questions?"

"You won't tell my dad about my hair, right?" This was the third time she had asked. "He doesn't know I have this problem and I don't want him to." Myra was being honest, so honest that she became afraid, uncomfortable, reached for her hair but instead sat on her hand, the metal chair frame cold against her knuckles.

"Don't worry," said Rachel. No smile, but her gaze was fixed on Myra. "We know how you feel."

"Okay."

"Your notes all ready?"

"Yeah." Myra had compiled them over the last three days, neat, numbered lists of all the whens and wheres and how muches. She was almost done reading them now, on page three of four. The lines on the notebook paper were pale blue, the color of clear sky. She had used a pen with green ink, green like grass, her letters loopless and straight compared to the handwriting of so many other girls. She didn't know why. She kept owning up, owning and owning, and her throat was beginning to throb, and Myra remembered the surgery, how she had fallen asleep so quickly after the anesthesiologist placed the mask over her face. Two nurses had looked down at her, eyes smiling, and said to count back from ten—then she woke up, her throat numb and her father not there because he had to teach, a nurse holding her hand as Myra wept with disorientation. The nurse brushed her forehead gently and gave her water to sip—*just a little*, she said, *your stomach might be queasy*—and told Myra where she was and why.

That's right. She was in Mercy Hospital, waiting to leave for Our Primary Purpose. She'd told Keen she would kill herself if he sent her to a treatment center. So he admitted her to Mercy on a suicide watch and then decided to get her that tonsillectomy Dr. Parrish had recommended to prevent Myra's chronic sinus infections. It made sense to do it now, since she would be in the hospital anyway. Two birds with one stone.

The nurse held her hand a little tighter. "The surgery went great."

"Okay," said Myra. She felt tears sliding sideways down her temples. Downhill.

"It went great. You are just fine."

"I think I need to sit up," Myra said.

"You have an IV in, honey. Let me help." The nurse put her hand under Myra's shoulders and helped her slowly upright.

"I'm going to throw up."

"Hold on, honey—just breathe. In and out. We're headed to the bathroom."

The nurse pushed the IV stand alongside Myra and held the tubing up and out of the way as Myra vomited. But because Myra was not allowed to eat before the surgery, what she was vomiting wasn't everyday vomit. It was a mixture of bile and stomach acid and water, a yellowish color, pale sunlit paint, and it shot out her nose and singed her fresh stitches.

"Lots of patients throw up after surgery," the nurse said, wiping Myra's mouth and forehead with a damp paper towel. "It's okay. You're going to be okay, honey."

But Myra held onto the metal bar drilled into the tiled wall by the toilet and kept heaving but expelling nothing, as if trying to rid herself of all she couldn't see. This sterile unsafe place, the raw fire in her throat, her own patheticness. All her wanting and wanting and wanting. Please go away. Please get out of my body. Please get out of my mind. Please tuck me in and let me feel your skin. Please take me into deep woods and grassy ancient plain and foreign jungle and show me what everything means.

But Myra would not tell them about all her desires. She was supposed to own up, and she had. She was done. And she was not crying. The conference room was silent as she looked up from her notes, swallowed, waited.

Her father was staring at her. He wore a jacket and a clean shirt and a tie. His huge hands were clasped together on the table.

"Keen," said Rachel. She wore a bright green collared shirt that day with white buttons. "Do you have questions? Anything you want to say to Myra?"

Keen pulled a handkerchief from his pants pocket, blew his nose loudly, put it back. No one spoke. Then he walked around the table and stood before Myra. He opened his long arms, spread them into an upside-down V, and attempted to smile.

"Do you have a hug for your father?"

"No physical contact yet, okay Keen?" said Russell Dean. "We wait until the end of Own Up."

Keen did not move, nor did he acknowledge that Russell Dean had spoken.

Myra stood up and hugged her father. He rested his arms around her in not a strong hug but a slight one, a hug that lacked firmness and presence. This was how he had always hugged her, not as if he didn't want to, but as if he didn't know how, didn't comprehend the protocol, didn't understand what was required.

But Myra hugged him with all of who she was, with every part of herself. Her throat hurt. She pressed her head into his significant chest and wrapped her arms around him. He was too big for the fingertips of her hands to touch; she pressed them into his back.

His tie felt cool against her cheek, his belly a place of rest, his giant frame a miniature mountain of safety.

Then he pushed her away, and she let him go. They returned to their seats and Myra grabbed Jen's hand and held it. Jen squeezed. Myra felt like Jen was her good, good friend. Keen blew his nose again. Myra gazed at him, wishing he would not leave, or that she could go with him.

"What would you like to say, Keen?"

Myra smiled at him limply. Her lips felt like wet noodles. He smiled back in the same way. She heard breath coming and going through his nose.

"I've been a bad parent," he said. And Myra's throat pain disappeared and switched to blankness, except it couldn't have been blankness because she could feel it and how could you feel nothing? Was this possible? What was in there?

"I don't think I can say much more right now."

"Would you like to write to her? Parents often take that option if they can't respond today."

"That might be the best thing," he said.

"Okay," Rachel closed a file folder. "There is something else we need to discuss before you go, Keen. We need to talk about Myra's hair-pulling."

Myra looked at Rachel and Rachel looked back slowly, her expression like a bare face of rock, as if she were looking down at Myra from a boulder, a cliff, an ancient platform of stone. Telling her how things would be. "We need to talk about this, Myra."

Myra felt herself breathing in. Breathing out. Her mouth hung open and she didn't know it.

Rachel smiled politely. "Myra acts on a compulsion to pull out her hair, Keen. She's been doing it since she was twelve. The medical term is Trichotillomania."

"You pull out your hair?" Keen stared at Myra, his eyes roaming over her head, all the barrettes and tiny buns swirled into place. He put his hands over his eyes and one of his long, thin hairs flopped over his left ear. Myra liked it when his hair fell out of its slicked hold. She liked seeing the curls he was always trying to comb away.

Jen's hand squeezed again. Myra's was limp. She wasn't angry. She was nothing.

"Myra, your father asked you a question." Russell Dean was looking at her now. He was intense, with narrow eyes, long hair, a wide jaw, and lips tight as stretched rubber bands.

Myra did not move her head but glanced over at Russell Dean and then back at the table, and then at her shirt, the way it rose and fell with each massive beat of her heart.

"We will help her with this, Keen," said Rachel. "The doctors are thinking of changing her medication. We can also help her figure out why she does it and help her control it."

Keen nodded, removed his hands from his face. "I… I'm… I'm sorry."

Myra looked up.

"I've been a bad parent," he said again. Looking at Myra.

"Do you have anything to say, Myra?" asked Rachel.

I want to see Nancy, she didn't say. Nancy had visited her after the tonsillectomy, that same afternoon when Myra had finally finished heaving and was lying in bed, watching the five-thirty rerun of *Hogan's Heroes*, the remote cool in her hand, her supper untouched.

"I brought you some ice cream," Nancy said, opening a small carton of Häagen Dazs. She wore that leather jacket all the time, even in summer. "I didn't know what you liked, so I just got vanilla."

"I don't know if I can eat it," Myra said. Her words were whispers.

"Sure you can, Sweetie. You got a spoon in here?" She lifted the metal cover over Myra's dinner and pulled out the spoon, rinsed it off, brought it to Myra, and watched television with her. She didn't talk about Cooper or about her mom. The only sounds Myra could hear were Hogan's chuckles and Sergeant Shultz's denials as slow, cool swallows of ice cream were sliding over the stitches and into Myra's empty, roiling stomach. Soothing it. Filling it up. Quieting things down. Until rehab, she could hide here. Tomorrow she could watch soaps, watch lovers move and live through houses and apartments and mansions so quiet and clean and safe. Even though they died. Even though they had split personalities and murdered people and blew up in boat explosions.

And she could pull out her hair as much as she wanted—just yank and yank and yank.

"I think we're done," said Rachel. "Jen, would you walk Myra back to the unit?"

"Of course," Jen said. She put her arm around Myra's shoulders and Myra noticed that she did not look at Myra's hair, did not scan her head for evidence of freakishness. Just a shoulder squeeze. "I'm here for you," she said.

Myra searched Rachel's face, her neck, her expression, her hands. Rooftops gleamed through the window behind her. Was it still the middle of the day? From a desk in one corner, the whole row of square plastic buttons on the phone were alight. Rachel shook Keen's hand and Myra searched a second more. A sentiment? A reaction? Her face was stone. Myra wished hers could be, too, strong and bare and revealing nothing instead of everything.

Fear

Jen was leading Community, twirling the long blue ribbon she wore to secure her ponytail around her index finger. The ribbon reminded Myra of *The Brady Bunch* and was cute with Jen's yoked and stonewashed baggie jeans, her OP sweatshirt. When Myra wanted new clothes—a few times a year—Keen wrote Myra a blank, signed check and gave her his driver's license so she could go to the Old Capitol Center or Sycamore mall. She had never taken Cindy or Nancy or anyone else because their confidence and surety made her feel split open, bare with trepidation between the dim, spotlit racks on the floor of Younkers or Maurices, where she flipped through racks of blouses with ruffled shoulders, pleated cropped pants, patterned sweaters that hung below hips. Whatever was popular. What did other girls wear? What did everyone like? If she stayed beneath the $100 limit Keen gave her, she would not be able to get more than two things, maybe three—but she needed lots and lots of new clothes so she could fit in. Which meant being noticed but not too much, being admired but not acting superior about it.

    Lisa with the straight bangs, drug of choice heroin, was staring at Billy, who was nearly finished sharing. Lisa's round cheeks were splotched red, and Myra knew she was terrified, so shy that she never shared in Community. But that morning in Small Group, Rachel had ordered her to.

"Share three feelings," Rachel had said to Lisa. "Then why you have them. You hide behind being quiet."

Patients were always fulfilling counselors' orders. No Contact if counselors discovered your relationship with another patient or if they thought your friendship was destructive. The Tuck-In Rule for slovenly dressers, usually for boys—but for girls if they thought you were ashamed of your body and trying to hide it. Nurturing, where you had to ask another patient to do all small tasks for you, like pull out and put away your meal tray, or open a bathroom door, light your cigarette.

"I'm Lisa," she said softly to Community. "And I'm an addict."

"Hi, Lisa," everyone said.

She sniffled and tried to smile. "I'm feeling nervous and scared and…" she looked at her hands. "Happy, I guess. Yeah. I don't live by the freeway anymore. And I won't ever go back, either."

It was warm, Lisa's feeling of safety. Myra felt it settle through the circle.

"I'm done."

"Thanks, Lisa," said Jen, who was replying to each patient, even though leaders were not supposed to. "I think you've let God in, finally. I was so scared for you."

Theresa and Tina rolled their eyes.

"I'm Victor," he said. Victor with the acne, drug of choice pot. He was beside Myra and even though she wasn't speaking, since all those eyes were almost on her, she felt suddenly the weight of her legs pressing into the chair, the heat in the back of her neck, the too-proper way her hands were resting in her lap. She sat on them. She was so self-centered. It wasn't *her* turn.

"Hi, Victor." He was just out of pajamas, tall and thin. He wore a blue bandana around his neck.

"I've been trying to pray," he said. "I want to let Him in, like Jen said. But then I picture that star." He shook his head. "And I can't. I just can't."

"What star?" Tina asked.

"The star of Satan," Jen said. She knew everything about everyone. Myra wondered if they liked this about her.

"I don't understand," Myra said, turning to look at Victor.

"I'm a Satanist," Victor said.

"You worship the devil?"

"Yeah," he said.

Myra scooted her chair backward. Out of the circle and away from him.

"What are you doing?" Jen asked.

"I can't sit next to him," Myra said. Myra remembered Prairie Lights bookstore when she was ten. She had sat on the floor, spun the rotating book rack, and picked out a black paperback. On the cover was a picture of a child illuminated by candles with a cackling, white-eyed face of a witch-man floating above. *Michelle Remembers*. The back said that her mother had been in a Satanic cult, the book an account of Michelle's memories of horrific abuse, human sacrifices, rituals of worship.

Her father had picked out *Double for Death* by Rex Stout and a thin, hardcover book of paintings by Picasso. Myra had read *Her Forbidden Knight*, always while on the couch in the living room to make sure Keen would see her reading it—but she took away only images of Wolfe sitting in his armchair or watering an orchid. That's what she told her father when he asked her what she made of it. He'd looked at her oddly and continued eating the fried chicken he had picked up from KFC. They picked up dinner several times a week.

Myra set *Michelle Remembers* on the checkout counter. Keen glanced down at it.

"Looks fine to me."

Myra had read the book quickly: Michelle on a table face down with a spike in her rectum. Michelle watching animal blood being poured on a baby. Every chapter ended with a moment of Satanic ritual and an exclamation point.

"All that stuff about evil and possession? That's all myth," Victor said. "It's just another religion. It's about freedom."

"Satanism is not what you think," Jen said. How did she know everything?

"It's okay," Charlie said. "Victor's cool."

"Come back into the circle, Myra," Jen said.

"No way."

"It's not like that!" Victor said. "I promise! That's all propaganda!"

"We can't have Community with you out of the circle," Jen said.

"She can trade places with me," said Billy.

They switched seats. Some of the others were smiling, but just as many were staring at Victor, shocked and open-mouthed.

After Community, they all put the chairs away and filed into the kitchenette to make Bedtime Snack.

"Victor's a great guy," Jen said. They stood at the study carrels. Myra crossed her arms and held them hard into her body.

"Satan is evil," Myra said.

"We don't drink blood or kill people," Victor said, walking up. "It's all political."

Ronald Reagan? Keen despised him. He had told Myra about trickle-down economics. "A beautiful con," he said. She remembered Carter losing and then the next election, watching TV with Keen when Mondale won only Minnesota, his home state blinking like a beacon in a map of red. At the end of his concession speech, Mondale waved from the podium and Keen had withered, a sunken man, his shoulders slumped as he stared at the screen.

"If democracy elects someone like Reagan, then to hell with it," Keen said.

Victor looked earnestly at Myra. "I'm trying to believe in God. I really am."

Myra remembered the vomit scene of *The Exorcist*, the way the possessed daughter trickled down the staircase in a backbend on her fingertips, looked sideways through the spindles. Her wrinkled, desiccated lips.

But Myra was trying to believe in God, too. Whenever she read a story of a redeemed alcoholic in the *Alcoholics Anonymous Big Book*, like "Freedom from Bondage" or "The Belle of the Bar," she tried to perceive God's will, read the declarations of devotion over and over again.

Victor put his hands in the pockets of his jeans, loose over his narrow hips. He had always seemed kind. Totally un-evil.

"Just give him a chance," Jen said.

"Okay," Myra said. Two other patients were making jelly sandwiches in the kitchenette, silverware clinking.

"Hug?" said Victor, opening his arms.

Myra did not want to hug Victor. Not at all. But she felt herself nod and consent to doing something she did not want to do. As he put his long arms loosely around her and patted her back, she smelled his aftershave. She wished she understood herself.

Dissent

Victor hated school. State-sponsored bullshit where jocks first learn to be oppressors. His econ teacher, Mr. Brooks, even had a Reagan picture framed on the back wall and a Republican elephant banner hanging down the side of his desk that faced the window so no other teachers could see it. Victor spent every class with his arms crossed and nothing on his desk, glaring.

"You want to get your book out, Victor?"

"Not really."

"Suit yourself, son."

Endless propaganda, that textbook. Every chapter a direct or indirect argument that supported supply and demand that Victor stopped reading after the first boring paragraph.

He came to every class after passing joints in the school parking lot, he and his friends in his van. It had been his father's, the vehicle his perfect parents had dated in, a 1970 Dodge, light blue with a thick white stripe above the tires. They sat on the overlapping rugs that covered the floor, a skull flag hanging over the back window and Black Sabbath on the stereo, Ozzy's voice like a chant. When they were done, the boys climbed out the rear doors and watched everyone watch them as smoke billowed out around them like an announcement. A grand emergence. An arrival. They coughed, pulled up the collars of their jean jackets. Smiled with closed mouths.

I DON'T CARE, Victor wrote in the blank for his name at the top of the first test, then sat back and closed his eyes. He thought he might fall asleep.

"Victor, let's talk in the hall," said Mr. Brooks. He was standing at Victor's shoulder, looking down at him. Creases pressed into his bald head.

Victor followed Mr. Brooks out of the room, adjusted the folded bandana he wore over his forehead, and tied at the back. He was dizzy. He needed to lie down.

"Why are you failing my class?"

"Am I?"

"Talk to me, son."

"That's okay."

"Are *you* okay? You don't seem well, son." He had a doughy nose. "You seem like you need some help."

"Don't call me son."

"I know your parents," he said. "We've been at city council meetings together. They're good people. What's wrong with you?"

"What are you talking about?" His parents would never speak to a man who had a picture of Reagan on his wall. Never.

"Son, are you *high*?"

Victor blinked quickly, a surge of fear. "Of course not."

"You're in big trouble."

"Please, Mr. Brooks."

"Son, I dabbled a little in the sixties. I'm no angel. But it is eight-thirty in the morning. And you are failing my class. And you are seventeen years old. You need help. I'm taking you to the principal's office."

"Like hell," Victor said, and he turned and walked down the hallway, past the lockers and the frosty glass panes in the classroom doors that made things hard to see. He went down the stairs and pushed the crossbar on the front doors way too hard and tingled with the resounding metal boom, the strike of the latch. The sidewalk stretched out before him: a line cut through the center of a miniature meadow of mowed grass.

Reagan. Chernobyl. South Africa. He wasn't the one who needed help.

Adapting

They moved Charlie to a room on the third floor, the girls' floor. Myra's floor. They had run out of rooms on the fourth, the main one for the whole unit, with a lounge and a nurses' station and counselor offices and double rooms for boys only. The new patient who had prompted Charlie's move was on suicide watch: no roommate allowed. He was now in Charlie's old room, door open at all times, right across from the nurses' station. From the correct angle, patients could see him lying in bed on his side, covered in a sheet from the waist down.

At dinner, Myra sat right across from him. Ron with the hazy eyes, drug of choice paint. She pictured three skinny teenagers in a garage huddled on their knees around a can of paint, sniffing and laughing. Was this how it worked? Why didn't she know this? Wasn't she an addict, too, because of her potential to be one?

"Ron, I'm glad you're here," she said, settling into the words, the rhythm of the greeting. She blushed and picked up her carton of milk and sipped it through the tiny red straw. Ron reminded Myra what it felt like to have thoughts of killing yourself. If someone had told her back then that she would be okay, she might have believed it, at least for a little while—until the thoughts had grown like dandelions in perfect squares of newly fertilized grass—

and then Myra had found herself lying in bed at night, reluctant to turn off her little black and white television, one hand on her gut beneath the covers and the other pulling out her hair. She didn't want to kill herself, exactly; Mark had broken up with her, and then thoughts of it had become so constant that she asked questions in response. Like *What if I did? Why am I thinking about it? Why can't I stop thinking about it?* She reassured herself: she was thinking about suicide in only a general way, like all human beings. But then she pictured ways she might commit suicide, if that's what she was actually thinking about, and she realized she was of course thinking about it, and that something was universally and deeply wrong with her. She might do it, that was one answer.

According to Keen, death was nothing. They'd been driving to Eagle's for groceries and Myra was trying to figure out how to get Keen to buy her Little Debbies, the vanilla cakes coated in chocolate with a layer of frosting in between. And then she asked.

"Where did Mom go?" Myra saw her mother in the offices of the university museum, walking down the hallway with office doors on either side of her while Myra sat at a desk punching an electric typewriter or coloring a picture on the carpeted floor.

"She's no place, Love," he said, flicking his cigarette butt out the window.

"Like being lost?"

"No. Death is… well, it's nothing. It's not a place. If we say she's lost, that implies that she can be found. She can't. We can't find her, and she can't find us. She's gone."

Myra blinked out the window. So her mother was looking for them, wandering the hills of the Earth with her hair blowing in the breeze, spindling around her.

"Does it hurt?"

"No, Love. It's just final."

Myra decided eventually that death was a return or re-entrance into nothing, into finality, a space blank and dismal and lonely, and the thought of entering such a world terrified her. But if she tried to kill herself, she would most likely fail, right? Because she would never see it all the way through. She wanted to live. She must. Come on! What were all these silly thoughts? And what would people think of a girl who tried to kill herself? If they didn't ridicule her, they would decide not to go near her, ignore her, because people found unstable girls disgusting. They had the potential to scare everyone away.

Myra put her fork down. Decided to try again. "Ron, really. I'm glad you're here." His hands were in his lap now; he stared at the space on the table between their trays. "They will take care of you. You are going to be okay."

"I don't know about that," he said.

During Smoke Break, Myra sat at one end of the table with Jen and Theresa. They wondered if Ron would be transferred to a psych ward.

"I hope so," said Theresa. She crossed her arms. She wore a Def Leppard T-shirt inside out, her forearms finally healing since she was no longer slicing herself with her fingernails—long and tough and unpolished, filed into points. "He's really weird. It doesn't seem like he belongs here."

"Um… that's not okay," said Jen.

"What's not?" asked Theresa.

"I mean, we all belong here," said Jen.

Theresa gazed at Jen for a few seconds, then lit a cigarette from the one she had just finished.

"Yeah, you're right." Theresa squashed the butt into the ashtray as the other patients started singing "Bad, Bad Leroy Brown," tapping the table softly to the beat.

Myra looked out the window, past the parking lot, at stoplights and gas stations and restaurants and hotels, signs sticking up into the air, way out to the end of all she could see, different heights and colors like a city section made out of blocks, like something a child might build. What had happened to Ron? Why had so many awful things happened to all of them? Myra did not feel like a kid, an adolescent, a young person. None of them did. They felt bruised, marred, wise with age, as if they had been living through the hardest parts of their lives. Some of them—maybe like Ron—felt used up. Finished with all the trying.

Charlie pulled up a chair and sat beside Jen.

"How's that no-sex contract going?" asked Jen.

"Shut up," said Charlie. Myra watched him smile at her, smiled back, looked at the ashtray. Bliss the tech leaned into the room and gave them the two-minute warning; Jen and Theresa put out their cigarettes and walked into the hallway.

Myra stared at Charlie. Did he have a girlfriend? Did he love her? This really wasn't okay, was it? That she wasn't strong enough to ask? She felt part of herself shrink.

"Want to meet in the bathroom after lights out?" Charlie asked softly.

"What?"

"I'm on your floor now, remember?"

Myra nodded. She smiled so hard she thought her face would split. She couldn't help it. She could see that he wanted to be with her. He was nervous. Sweat beaded in the hairs on his upper lip.

So that night Myra waited in her room, lying in her bed with the covers up and Winnie the Pooh on her desk—it was too crackly to sleep with—and the lights out, her door left open the required two inches. From one wall to the other, the ceiling was rectangles framed in metal. What the rectangles were made of, she did not know, but in the light of day they appeared soft, like foam you could leave marks in with your fingertips, and you could see pale specks of gray. She still had no roommate. Girls often didn't, since boys outnumbered them by three to one. Charlie's new room was separated from the girls by the bathroom and a dimly lit nurses' station where no one did any nursing. The station was for the graveyard technician, usually Erin, a tiny woman with wiry blond hair and large frameless glasses. She stayed at the desk all night, there for anyone who approached her. Jen talked to her after lights out, sat beside her with her *Big Book* open and a pencil in her hand. Myra heard wisps of their conversations as she fell asleep—the Twelve Steps, acceptance, humility, why resentments made alcoholics drink. Myra could tell Erin had been through hell. She seemed sad, strangely quiet. Jen said yeah, she had been through hell, but Erin had twelve years sober and she was serene—solid and at peace. And when Jen put it that way, Myra saw Erin's serenity, too, in the way she looked at you so intently and seriously whenever you spoke to her about anything—a towel you couldn't find or a boyfriend who betrayed you or an aunt who kept you locked in a basement for three days when you were seven. Erin was all there. Myra had come to realize that serenity looked different on everyone.

And she wanted it.

Imagine not caring what other people thought of her. Imagine loving herself. Imagine not being afraid.

As she walked past Erin at the non-nurses' station to meet Charlie, Myra was in hospital pajamas, as patients were required to be at night, the material as thin as her father's tired handkerchiefs. Charlie was in hospital pajamas, too—all white, with a V-neck shirt, almost like scrubs. But in the light that shone through the darkness from the windows above them, his pajamas looked blue, the air looked misty. Charlie was leaning against the washing machine, his penis jutting out beneath his pants. Myra had felt a wash of something—fear? shame? pleasure?—but as soon as he saw her he reached for her and pulled her to him without embarrassment. Myra thought she might love him. They made out, mouths and lips moving in steady, rhythmic circles, tongues exploring, muscles tightening and relaxing. He reached down and squeezed Myra's ass and she pressed herself into him and felt the solidity and size of him against her. Her underwear was soaked—she had felt the first surge of wetness on her way down the hall. He moved his hands up her back and over her ass again and they kissed and kissed and then he moved his hands around to her stomach, reached beneath her waistband, touched the space below her belly button with the backs of his fingers.

"Tina?" Erin called another patient from down the hallway.

They jumped and separated.

"Don't you need to get your laundry?" Erin called.

They leaned on the washing machine, damp hands clutching stainless steel.

"I got it before," Tina called.

"Go back," he whispered. "Go back."

Myra ran over and flushed a toilet, then passed Erin on the way back to her room.

"Good night, Myra." Erin smiled, looking up from behind the counter.

"Good night." Myra smiled in return, wondering if Erin could hear her heart beating, a steady throb, the kind that made Myra euphoric and shut out all her despair.

But Myra and Charlie had to be careful. When he walked into Community for breakfast the next morning, she did not look at him and he did not acknowledge her. Myra pulled her tray from its row in the food cart and sat down on the opposite end of the table from him, lifted the dome off her plate, smelled the melty white toast. Was he ignoring her because he didn't want them to get caught, or was he ignoring her because their relationship was over and he no longer liked her? Had she done something wrong? How was she supposed to know what he was thinking if they could never talk? She couldn't reveal their relationship to Jen or anyone—Jen would probably tell on her because relationships were not allowed. They interfered with recovery. Patients who had them got a restriction: No Contact—no eye or physical or verbal contact with the other patient. Or they lost Smoke Breaks. Or desserts. Or both. Sometimes they got kicked out. And by Day Ten or Fifteen, most of the patients wanted to stay and get better, get well, not use anymore. A lot of them didn't want to leave at all. They feared Day Sixty, when they would have to return to The Outs. How could they stay sober and how could they possibly live in their families again? They would have to earn trust, obey strict curfews and rules. Some patients didn't have to go home—they went to halfway houses for six months or a year or two years, and then maybe into foster homes. That's what Lisa would do since returning home, where her cousin still lived, was not an option. The patients who did return, some with over-protective families and some with abusive families and some with disengaged families, would have to do whatever their parents instructed—and then turn away their using friends. Who might also be their best friends since childhood. And if they didn't go to Alcoholics Anonymous or Narcotics Anonymous meetings and work their programs, they were doomed. Done for. *Jail, insanity, or death*, they all said. These were the only possible outcomes for the using addict, the practicing alcoholic. Jail, insanity, death. The only three items on the biggest list of all time.

    Charlie was on Day Thirty; when he was done, he would go home. His drug of choice was LSD. His favorite band was Rush. Just as he looked up from his eggs and winked, Myra realized she was staring at him. She looked away and ate her toast. So he did still like her. Why couldn't she be cool like him? Like everybody else? Why did she have to doubt his feelings for her when they were so obvious—especially after last night? After the drawing he made of her? Why did she have to be such an insecure girl? She should turn it over, work Step Three—give her insecurity to God. She wanted to pray. To stop eating and close her eyes and clasp her hands together, put them on her forehead so God would know she was serious.

But in front of Charlie? In front of everyone? No way. She would do it later.

***

Myra got her diagnosis that morning—she was chemically dependent and she would be there for sixty days. Tina, Theresa, Jen, and Lisa all stared at her. And there was a new girl, Abbey with the hair that wouldn't feather, drug of choice cocaine. She wore the required pajamas and a squint full of wrath.

Myra reached for her hair.

"Put your hand away," Rachel said. Myra dropped it into her lap. "Leave your hands there. A restriction for you is that you have to sit on your hands during group. Any group. That means in here or in Community."

"They'll fall asleep," Myra said. Her face burned.

"Wiggle your fingers. That will help."

Fine, Myra didn't say. I'll do it after lights out. I'll pull it all out if I want to. She gazed into the middle of the circle because she got to do that, too.

Rachel leaned back in her chair. She got one with arms. "What do you have to say, Myra?"

Myra did not want to return to City High. So much pressure, so many girls who were uninterested in her and boys she didn't know how to talk to and activities she wasn't brave enough to try. She wanted to be in a play, but she was too afraid to join. What would they all think? Drama club? When Mark had been her boyfriend, his popularity was a cover. She walked through the loud hallways with confidence. Mark's girlfriend. But without him Myra felt even less comfortable than before they had been together, almost panicked. She walked past lockers and open classroom doors and around girl-and-boy clusters that seemed to her perfectly formed, like struggle-free organisms. Her fears removed her, set her apart.

Myra did not want to return to her own house, either, an ailing two-story box with an unfinished basement, brown and orange blobbed carpet, stale walls. Its emptiness left her with a vacant flatland of dread that made her head heavy with apparitions of interstates and cornfields, of rich topsoil that she had learned in fourth grade was quickly eroding, of tired pioneers that she felt no connection to. Of the mother she did not have and wanted so much.

"Hand me that chimney," her mother said one night before dinner. They were building something with tiny wooden logs on the floor of Myra's room, their legs crisscross applesauce, Myra's Winnie the Pooh tucked into the triangle of her folded legs. She had never read the books and knew none of the stories but that disconnected bear was her favorite.

Myra never recalled what they built together—the structures and places disappeared, never fully formed or populated. Had they been making a doll-cabin? So much vanished. Myra did not remember what had existed or comprehend what might have been.

But most of all, she did not want to leave Charlie. She thought of him all day and felt secret waves of what she thought was love whenever he entered a room.

Myra offered a smile. "I'm glad I'm here."

Except for Abbey with the hair that wouldn't feather, drug of choice cocaine, the faces in the circle smiled back. Even Rachel's. She had wide gums.

"Glad you're here," they said. And she knew they meant it but thought about Charlie instead of that.

Veracity

Jen knew she had to tell Rachel about her brother. Jen had to tell her everything so that she could get sober and get well. She asked Rachel not to tell her parents.

At Jen's Own Up, Rachel told them anyway.

"In the years following the divorce, there was some sexual acting out between Jen and Jeremy."

So that was all it had been. A mutual thing, a curiosity thing. Well, okay! What a relief! But was that relief? She couldn't tell how she felt. A little knocked in the head, like she'd been hit with something but not in a specific spot. She became aware that she was breathing.

Jeremy was there, too. Six years older than Jen, now twenty-one. He and her father both looked at their shoes and shifted positions while her mother looked at Jen with strange eyes and started to cry. She looked sick. Why? It had just been a little acting out, apparently. Jen had willingly participated, apparently. Right? Nothing had happened *to* her. Nothing was like she thought it was. What a relief! She felt it and held on.

"What do we do?" asked her mother.

"Today, Jen needs to own up," said Rachel. "After you leave today, you'll have to talk about what you think you should do."

"You might want to consider family therapy after Jen finishes treatment," said Russell Dean.

"For all of us?" said her mother. "We've been divorced for eight years."

"We can discuss options later this week," said Rachel. "You ready, Jen? Let's get started."

Jen looked down at her legal pad and tried to speak, to begin, but she didn't know where the beginning was anymore. The starting line had moved from her first lie to before then, a long way back. Not necessarily to other lies, but other starts. Were they the same thing, a lie and a start? She tried to speak and could not.

"Are you okay?" Theresa asked. She was Jen's peer support. She put her hand on Jen's shoulder.

"No physical contact, please," said Russell Dean.

Theresa glared at him and took her hand away. "Why don't I get her some water."

"I think she's ready," said Rachel.

Jen didn't start to cry, which surprised her. You'd think after that reveal, she'd be uncontrollable! Oh my God! But no. She just couldn't speak. Never happened to her before, this weird lump without tears to follow. She was confused, but then she took a breath, found her voice, and started confessing. It felt wrong but she did it anyway, tamped down her objections like a child playing on a pile of leaves in the fall.

Plans

After they were diagnosed, patients could receive mail. They crowded around the nurses' station every day at one-thirty, waiting for Grace and Bliss to remove letters from their envelopes, press them out against the desk as if they were trying to iron them, and hand them over the counter one at a time to each patient. Myra was on Day Eighteen and had received no mail yet, but she had written to Nancy, so maybe Nancy had written her back. Or she might get that letter from her father. Or maybe a letter from Cindy, with whom Myra had stopped spending time when she'd started dating Mark. Instead of going to Mazzio's Pizza with Cindy after football games that the Little Hawks played every Friday, Myra waited for Mark in his car so they could go to his house, watch TV in his basement, make out, and dry hump until he came. Instead of going downtown to the Old Capitol Center Mall with Cindy on Saturdays, Myra went to Mark's house to watch TV in his basement, make out, and hump until he came. But maybe Cindy had forgiven Myra for blowing her off, written her a letter with fluffy kittens in the margins just to say hi, that she couldn't believe how sad it was that Myra was in there. Maybe people missed her, people she didn't expect. Maybe some of those older popular girls who were friends with Mark had sent her a little postcard or something. Or even Chad Norris. Why not? Wasn't he a human being? Anyone could reach out—you never knew. Maybe he felt guilty for something and wrote a hello. Just a friends thing.

Grace and Bliss were pressing out the last two letters. Grace handed one to Tina.

"Who's the last one to?"

"Not you," said Bliss.

"Sorry," said Grace. "Nothing today either, Myra."

"Okay." Myra walked down the hall. Beside her, Lisa held four letters.

"Who writes to you?"

"Friends," Lisa said. They sat down on the hallway carpet outside Rachel's office to wait for afternoon group to start. "When I was homeless, I met a lot of people. This one is from my brother, though. And this one—" she brushed bangs from her eyes and squinted. Myra could tell the handwriting was a boy's—boxy, unslanted.

"This one is from… oh wow. It *is* from my ex." Lisa not only had lots of friends, she had lots of friends who cared about her. Lisa had a presence that pulled people in, a magnetic draw. She was very real, very honest, unafraid and confident. She didn't attempt to say the right things, and it didn't seem to Myra that she did anything to get attention—she just got lots of it all the time. And Myra liked Lisa—she liked Lisa a lot—but she thought these opposing conditions of existence were unfair, that if you didn't want attention and love you got lots of both, and if you wanted attention and love you got very little of either. Or maybe Myra could not feel and appreciate all the attention she already received because of her low self-esteem. Rachel had told her this before. So had Judy. She had looked it up in the gigantic Merriam-Webster dictionary in the City High library that sat on a swivel podium: "confidence in one's worth or abilities; self-respect."

Where was *that* supposed to come from? Would it just emerge with Elavil and therapy? It hadn't so far. Would it eventually make itself known? Maybe Myra could act-as-if. Jen had said this the other day about God, that when she didn't believe, she acted as if she did.

Myra closed her eyes and felt the hallway wall against her back. What would she be doing right now if she had self-esteem? She wouldn't be jealous of all the other girls' letters. Okay. She tried to will the jealousy away.

Rachel opened her office door, stuck her head out. "Just one more minute," she said, closing the door again. She was conferring with Russell Dean. They always did before groups.

"What do you think she's going to do?" Myra asked Jen and Tina. They were sitting across the carpet, reading letters. Myra was not saddened by this at all.

"Oh, she has a plan," said Tina. Her teeth were spaced apart so strangely that it affected her speech, but she was speaking more and more and caring less and less about her impediment. Myra was proud of her. "Maybe they learned something new about you and want to confront you. Or maybe it won't be your turn after all. They change plans without saying anything sometimes. It could be any of us."

"But you haven't been up in a while," Jen said. "I bet it is you, Myra."

"Shit," Myra said fiercely. She pretended she didn't love being the center of attention because the thought of being honest about this felt like she was violating something; but when she did pretend, the guilt made her feel like a fraud. Phony and finky, the word Keen used to describe Gary Hart.

What a shit sandwich.

Jen looked down at her letter again and Myra's jealousy returned. Myra had to accept that she could not feel the love of others because she did not love herself! She had heard this many times since she got here, one of so many proclamations that echoed through the rooms. But for this to be true, wouldn't more people have to befriend and adore her? Didn't Lisa feel loved and confident because she got so many letters? How was Myra supposed to feel the love of others if no one wrote to her, if no one reached out to her? Maybe Myra was generally unlovable. Yes. She knew this. And also uninteresting and boring. And these truths scared people away. And her wanting made people sick. Myra often made herself sick. Look at the way she had waited like a sad toy animal at the nurses' station, fantasizing about all the mail she might get. No one would believe her if she tried to explain her unlovability. They would just tell her she had low self-esteem.

Not everyone did. Low self-esteem was not a giant patient-blanket. Yesterday had been Abbey's Tell-All, and that isn't what Rachel had said at all.

"So after I got out of the hospital," Abbey said, "my parents told me I couldn't see Keith anymore. So I ran away."

"You put your parents through hell," said Jen.

Abbey shrugged.

"You don't care?" said Theresa.

Abbey shrugged again.

"So self-centered," said Jen. "So sick."

"They might be the only ones who really care about you," said Rachel.

"Keith loves me." Keith was twenty-three, Abbey seventeen.

"Keith is an addict, Abbey," said Rachel. "He's not capable of loving you."

Abbey rolled her eyes. "Yeah, right."

"He still used with you after last year?" Lisa asked.

"I'm the one who started again."

"What do you think he's doing while you're in here?"

"Waiting for me to get out so we can smoke a joint." Abbey smiled.

Rachel leaned forward. "You understand that I don't give a shit?"

Abbey's smile shrank.

"No one gives a shit what you do, Abbey, except for your parents, who won't for much longer. And then what?"

Abbey was wearing shorts and looked at her knees. One of them had an old, yellowed bruise spread over the kneecap.

"If you want to use again, you can," Rachel said. "No one really gives a shit what you do. These girls do, while you're here—but after they graduate, they'll be working on their own recoveries."

Rachel paused. Rachel always paused.

"People aren't paying attention like you think. Addicts don't get this. They are inherently self-absorbed. It's part of your disease."

"I'll be eighteen in November."

"Your parents will have kicked you out by then. Maybe Keith will be dead. Addicts die every day."

A tear dripped onto Abbey's thigh.

"As you know."

Drip.

"Were you scared when you almost died?"

Drip.

"Answer me."

"I don't know."

"I do. You were scared out of your mind. But instead of talking about it, you lashed out. Who else lashes out when they're afraid?"

Theresa, Lisa, Jen, Tina, and Stephanie raised their hands, so Myra did, too.

"Addicts' lives can go three ways," said Rachel. "Jail, insanity, or death."

Myra watched the other girls nod.

"With your history, you'll get to one of those pretty soon," said Rachel. She leaned back in her chair, crossed her legs, folded her hands together, kept her eyes right on Abbey.

"And Abbey, honestly, if you keep going like this, I don't think you'll live to twenty."

Abbey's eyes were still down.

"Look at me," said Rachel.

"No."

"Look at me."

Abbey looked up, face splotched. She seemed worn out.

"And that will be your choice."

In the hallway, Abbey sat away from them as she always did. Rachel opened her office door and looked down at the girls. Lisa and Tina put their letters in their pockets.

"Come on in," Rachel said from over their heads.

The girls sat down. The fluorescent ceiling light was on for some reason, making Rachel's office artificially bright.

***

In sixth grade, Myra had run away.

It was during school—twelve-thirty, right after lunch, a beautiful April day in Iowa City. Myra asked Mr. Zuelke if she could go to the bathroom, and when he said yes, she walked out of the room and down the hall and the three flights of tiled stairs and directly out the front door of Horace Mann Elementary School. She had a ten-dollar bill in the back pocket of her jeans, white tennis shoes with thick socks, an orange windbreaker with light lining. She was planning to hitchhike to San Francisco to live with her friend who had moved away the year before because now she had no friends and she was sick of it. She felt brave. She walked down Church Street as fast as she could. In her ears the sound of her breathing and the beats of her heart were louder than the tires on the asphalt—or was it concrete, cement, pavement, aggregate? What was the difference among all those materials?

Myra did not look back. She was taking control. On her way.

***

"So how you doing, Myra?" Rachel asked. Why was that light on? It had always been off.

"Fine," she said. "I'm glad I'm here. Glad I'm sober."

"Really?"

Myra nodded.

"What do you all think?" Rachel looked at the others. "Do you think Myra's glad to be sober?"

"She never talks about it," Tina said.

"No, she doesn't," said Jen. "I love you, Myra. But you don't talk about your program."

"How does it feel to be sober?" Rachel asked.

"Fine."

"Let's talk about the First Step. You remember what it is?"

"That I'm powerless over alcohol."

"And that your life has become unmanageable."

"Right."

"Do you feel powerless over alcohol, Myra?"

Myra reached for her hair.

"Now *there's* something you're powerless over."

Myra's hand stopped for a second, and then she twirled hair around her index finger.

"You going to pull it out?" Rachel asked.

Myra exhaled and felt fire rising in her cheeks.

"Unwrap it."

She panted, tried to catch air.

"You can do it, Myra. Don't you think she can unwrap it, everyone?"

"Yes! You can do it!" They all said something like that, broken up and in unison, a series of what sounded to Myra like the quacks of ducks. She wasn't sure what they were saying or what they really meant. She felt those hairs around her finger, the way they cut so delicately into her skin. She salivated.

"Unwrap them," Rachel said. "Just let it go, Myra. It's okay."

Myra swallowed. Tears came. She couldn't do it. She wanted to die. She wanted to hide for the rest of her life.

But she felt herself put her hand in her lap. She sniffled. Tears dripped onto her collar bone. One splattered onto her shirt.

"No Kleenex allowed," Rachel said. "Feel those tears." And she leaned forward, put her elbows on her knees. She had a tip of booger hanging out her left nostril. "That was great work. Good job."

"Good job, Myra," they all said, and Myra believed them.

***

The walk along Church Street and then Dubuque, toward Interstate 80, was hot and sweaty, but she was too nervous to take off her windbreaker. It hung to her knees, so oversized that it hid her body, and if she made her body visible, men might eye her or want to pick her up. But wasn't this what she wanted? To be picked up and taken to San Francisco? Yes. Just not until the Interstate.

She had to get out there first and walk awhile. Then she would start hitchhiking.

As Myra passed the fraternity mansions along the Iowa River and crossed the Park Road bridge, the breeze turned to wind. By the time she reached I-80, the wind whipped her open windbreaker around her. She stood on the overpass and watched the cars beneath her and then leaned over the concrete parapet to wait for a semi—a giant bullet of monolith that would shoot out right under your face, right under your body. You could feel it in the bottoms of your feet. If you weren't expecting it, you might scream. Myra didn't, but she let herself be afraid with the passing of each one, and then she looked out over the band of highway through Iowa, the clusters of trees, the gleam of the sun. Without the highway, what would be here? What would things look like? It all used to be prairie—this she knew—way back before she was born, before her father was born, before her mother had been born and then killed on a highway. Myra let herself think of her mother, let the wind bring her. Then Myra wondered if things would look the same in California, if the EXIT signs would still be green. She tied her wind breaker around her waist—it would still cover her lower half—and walked to the end of the overpass and down the hard gravel shoulder of the acceleration ramp.

***

"Do you think you're powerless over pulling out your hair?" Rachel asked.

Sniffle. Exhale. "I don't know."

"At the very least—" Rachel reached behind her and took the box of Kleenex from the corner of her desk. "You know what you *think*, right? So you can tell us that." She held up the Kleenex. "And you can have one of these after all." She passed the box to Abbey, who handed it around the circle. Myra took one and wiped her neck, her nose.

"Time to have a Think. Three minutes. We'll wait."

That light was driving Myra nuts.

***

She wasn't holding her thumb the right way. In two miles of walking Myra had held it out twice, her hand out there in the wind with her thumb up in the air, and she felt ashamed, embarrassed—everyone would know she didn't know how to hitchhike. From across the median a few semis had honked their air horns. She must have looked older than she was, especially since no one could see her face. Myra started feeling her breasts jiggle, just a little, in her training bra, the one that she had bought in the Old Capitol Mall at Younkers while her father waited on the bench outside Cookies & More.

"You get it taken care of?" he asked when she returned with her shopping bag.

She nodded.

He held out his hand. "Let's go."

She didn't take it. She had stopped taking his hand ages ago. She walked away from him.

A white Buick pulled over in front of her, its back bumper missing and all its windows down. Strange for someone to stop—she hadn't had her thumb out—and she decided not to get in anyone's car if she hadn't been asking for a ride. This decision seemed wise.

"Can I give you a lift?" The driver had to shout in the wind, in the vrooms from all those engines.

"I don't think so!" she shouted back.

"Where you going?" He seemed so far from her, all the way across the bench seat, his hair curly and wild, Iowa endless behind him.

"San Francisco!"

"And you don't want a ride?"

She shook her head. "Thanks anyway!"

"You just want to walk out here?"

"Yes!"

"Okay, honey! Be careful!" He drove off, dust rising. Myra looked up at the SPEED LIMIT 55 sign over her head. The surface of the sign was actually rough, dotted, not smooth as it appeared from a car window. And it was tall, taller than her father, higher than the ceilings in her house. She had had no idea how big everything was out here—the green EXIT signs in the grass outside the shoulder were huge and swayed in the wind, the white letters textured with tiny reflective circles, dirty and smeared and smudged with probably the same grime that was settling into the palms of Myra's hands. She felt small and out of place, as if she were a character who had been dropped into a bizarre set, but she also felt like she was gaining knowledge. So this is what signs on a highway look like. This is what they really are. Had anyone ever seen them so close up before? She wished she could reach them. Myra scratched her scalp. It was gritty. Her hair must be a mess. She held a thick lock of it in front of her eyes and rubbed it between her fingers. The ends had become brittle and dry, stiff and weirdly shiny. She was thirsty.

***

"I don't know how to answer you," Myra said finally. Rachel told Abbey to stop biting her cuticles and Theresa to keep her hands still—she'd had a slip with cutting the day before. Told Tina to blow her nose.

"Just now, did you know you were reaching for your hair?"

Myra shook her head.

"Do you think you can stop?"

Myra shrugged.

"Alcohol is the same way. You're powerless over it."

But you reach for it and drink it, Myra didn't say. You pick up a can or a bottle and you put it to your mouth and drink it. How could anyone be powerless over an action like that? Over an object, a thing, something external from you? That doesn't make any sense.

"Jen," Rachel said. "Tell Myra what powerless means."

"You just have to admit it," Jen said. "Once you admit it, it's not that bad. Then you can get better."

"I think you should write about something, Myra," said Rachel. "I want you to make two columns." She held up her hands to illustrate. "Call one column 'I am powerless over,' and call the other column 'I am not powerless over.' Then report back to us tomorrow."

Myra knew that some assignments and report-backs didn't get shared. There might be a new patient to deal with, or someone might bring up an issue. So Myra simply nodded.

It was now Abbey's turn. Again. They were spending a lot of time on her. She was so angry, so defiant. There was respect in that.

"And ask for help, okay?"

"Sure," said Myra.

***

The Ramada's bar was backed with solid mirror and clear shelves lined with liquor bottles almost up to the ceiling. Myra looked at her reflection. She was dirty, her hair almost spiky because the wind had blown out the Aqua Net. She couldn't see her face very well, her reflection wedged among all those bottles. How would she make money? She had thought that a nice trucker like the one in the episode of *Charlie's Angels*, when Kris and Tiffany go to trucking school, would pick her up and just… take care of her. Buy her some food, let her sleep on a soft pad he kept in the sleeper cab. She was only a child, all alone out here. Wouldn't they feel sorry for her? Want to help?

Myra climbed onto a barstool, the seat covered in a soft red fabric. Suede? Velour? Velvet. She was sure of it. "How much is a Coke?" she asked.

"One dollar," said the bartender, a heavy woman in jeans and a T-shirt, bangle earrings swinging.

"Can I have one?"

"Sure, honey." She placed a skinny frosted glass full of ice—each cube a clear, perfect square except for that half-moon on one side—in front of Myra and filled it up with Coke from the bar gun. Myra drank it.

"Can I have another one?"

"Just a sec," she said. She didn't look up, busy chopping lemons.

The bartender filled Myra's glass. "Be another buck."

"No refills?"

"Nope."

Her ten-dollar bill was sweaty and limp as she handed it over. She didn't meet the bartender's eye as she took her change, uncomfortable, afraid she was suspicious. Myra hopped down, walked through the bar and out to the parking lot to cut across the tall, rough grass toward the interstate. Her feet hurt. She was sure that a mile out here was longer than it was elsewhere.

She was walking for only a few minutes when Myra heard tires crunching the gravel shoulder behind her. A police car approached, lights rotating, sirens silent. He wore mirrored sunglasses and his shirt was light blue. He didn't smile at all, and when he asked for Myra's name she chose not to lie, although she thought about it at first and even stammered because she was bad at lying and she knew it, and even if she did lie, wouldn't he figure it out? He was a cop. Isn't that what they did?

He held the CB microphone to his lips and spoke Myra's name. Something was confirmed—a man's voice through the radio—and the officer led her into the backseat, where Myra gazed at all the equipment on the dashboard.

On the way back to Horace Mann—this is where he had to take her, he explained, because school was still in session, as it wasn't yet three o'clock—Myra thought about what might have happened if she had been hit by a semi today. She'd been picturing the consequences of her getting in an accident since she was a tiny child, since she was aware of her ability to think, to possess memories. Maybe Myra would get paralyzed—not from the neck down, just from the waist down—and return to school in a wheelchair, her hair woven into beautiful French braids by a nurse in a hat and white uniform who took care of her. Or maybe Myra would have been killed. Would she get to watch their reactions? Maybe when you died it wasn't nothing. Maybe you got to hover and observe, invisible from a spot in a corner of the ceiling. Maybe you finally had a chance to learn what other people were thinking. Maybe all your questions got answered—not just about materials and flowers and trees and prairie and civilization but about how the world viewed you. Where you were placed. How you were categorized. Maybe if she died Myra would get to watch her own funeral. Would the girls at school weep with regret, standing around her coffin holding flowers to their chests, surrounded by wreaths and grief and soothing dark curtains that covered the walls? Would they realize what they had lost in neglecting her?

School was just getting out when they arrived at Horace Mann; the officer led Myra past all the gawking children on the front stairs and Myra kept her eyes down, her cheeks hot with shame. But she was grinning. She saw herself and tried to stop but could not, the muscles in her jaw solid as stone.

Maybe they would pay attention to her now.

Keen, the principal, and the vice-principal were waiting for her in the office. Skirts, slacks, low pumps. Gray walls behind them. Painted cinderblocks.

"Thank God," Keen said, despite his non-belief, pulling her to him. She pushed him away.

Two girls from her class peeked in, smiling just a little. Were they being nice or mean? Myra smiled back.

"Shoo!" said the principal. Her hair was gray and short, sprayed into something like curls.

"The city police and sheriff were looking for you," said the vice-principal. She held a pale file folder. "You scared us to the moon."

"Let's go," said Keen, putting his hand on her shoulder.

"Can we please wait until all the other kids go home?" Myra asked.

"Nope," said the vice.

"Yes," said Keen. "Of course we can."

Myra nodded, sniffled. Myra did not understand. She was good almost all the time. Wasn't being good and kind and thoughtful—caring for others and wanting them to care about you—shouldn't this be the path to happiness? Wasn't it? The way to become a person whom everyone would love?

***

Charlie put his hand, very gently, into Myra's underwear. She felt his finger slide in and she inhaled urgently, louder than she had intended, grabbed him by the back of his head. She pressed his kiss into hers, moved herself forward on his finger.

"Shh!" Charlie said. He pulled his hand out. They stood against the washing machine and clutched its edge, the way they always did after a few minutes, when something made them stop. They waited. No sound. He put his arms around her waist. In the moonlight she could see the pocks of faded acne in his cheeks, the length of his eyelashes, soft and lush. Behind him, mirrors lined a row of sinks.

"You want to run away?" he asked. "They can't kick us out if we come back within twenty-four hours." He squeezed her ass. "I just want to be with you. So much."

"Me, too."

"If we're not back in twenty-four, we're automatically out."

"I don't want that," Myra said.

"Me neither. I just want to be with you."

Myra nodded, kissed him, listened to the whispers of his plan.

Boys, Crying

Rachel was home sick, so that afternoon they combined the two Small Groups into one. Billy, the senior patient, was up. Instead of going home in four days, he would go to a halfway house in Ames for one year. And like all patients who were soon getting out, he had several assignments to complete—resentments to overcome, character defects to expunge, amends to offer. On Day Fifty-eight or Fifty-nine, Billy would admit to God, to himself, and to another human being the exact nature of his wrongs. This was the Fifth Step of the Twelve Steps that you worked in Alcoholics Anonymous. You could do your Fifth Step with whomever you wanted, and Billy had chosen not Russell Dean but Travis the tech. If Billy had wanted to do it with someone outside the unit that would have been fine, too. Counselors could call in an Old-Timer from the program, a priest or a minister, whomever the patient wanted. But before anyone could leave OPP, the Fifth Step had to be done—and in order to give one, every patient had to first complete the Fourth Step—a searching and fearless moral inventory where you wrote down every bad thing you had ever done. Every resentment you had. Everything that you felt guilty about. Or not.

Patients wrote their Fourth Steps on lined notebook paper, using as many pages as it took and always comparing the extent of their wrongs. *Mine's five pages. Mine's ten. Mine's twenty-three. But did you use both sides? Did you write on every line or every other line?*

But Billy wasn't sharing his inventory—that wasn't appropriate at group level. He was reading from a list he had made about why he never asked for help, or something like that; Myra wasn't sure because she was sitting in Small Group with Charlie for the first time and she had to act like nothing was happening between them, and whether she avoided looking at Charlie or looked at Charlie their relationship would be obvious. As Billy spoke, Myra was attempting not to sweat, to calm herself, to quiet her heartbeat. Russell Dean's office was right next to Rachel's, the view out his windows the same as hers—closed blinds of the adjacent building.

She reached for her hair.

"Where's your hand, Myra?"

Russell Dean spoke to her without moving his gaze from the center of the circle or moving at all. Billy stopped talking. They all looked at Myra. Around her index finger she had coiled a few hairs from that tender place on the back of her neck; her teeth were clenched to prepare for the force, that rush of removal that felt like change, like something new.

"I asked you where your hand is," he said. Russell Dean had a wide mouth.

Myra unwrapped the hairs and compelled her jaw to relax. She felt as if something had deserted her, left her, abandoned her. Something important was abruptly unfinished, a crucial process ruptured.

"You have a restriction. Please sit on your hands." Still not looking at her. She stared at his profile, the way his chin jutted out. "Don't move them for the rest of group."

Myra did as he asked, felt the squish of her thighs keeping her fingers in place, flesh protecting her from herself. Would Charlie think she was unstable now? Would he be afraid of her? Maybe not; maybe he would understand; maybe in the haze of bathroom moonlight he would hold her and tell her he loved her no matter what.

"Good work, Billy," said Russell Dean. "Last word?"

"Sure," said Billy. He was lanky and lean, with skeletal fingers and bony shoulders and a deep voice. "I don't like asking for help because I think I can do it all myself. I think I can handle things."

"Handling things got you in here," said Sam with the bleached hair but brown eyebrows, drug of choice pot.

"I know."

"Do you, Billy?" said Russell Dean.

"Definitely."

Russell Dean nodded his head. "For one of the first times since you showed your skinny face in here, I believe you. I think you're being honest. I think this is new."

Billy scrunched his mouth and nodded.

"How does it feel?"

Billy sighed and teared up. Myra had never seen a boy cry before. Never once in her whole life except for toddlers on playgrounds.

"Okay."

"No, it doesn't," Russell Dean said. "Try again."

"Scary as shit."

"That's right," said Russell Dean, and his eyes met Billy's. "You're right where you need to be. Just let it in. You're okay, man. Victor, pass Billy a tissue."

Victor had just returned from running away; the police had found him and brought him back. He wore pajamas, a five-day consequence for running. He looked exhausted. Was he high? Myra didn't trust herself enough to tell. But he passed the Kleenex wearily to Billy. He did what he was told. Who wouldn't? What did Russell Dean do if someone said no, if someone never came around? Was there a dungeon?

Billy wiped his nose and sat back in his chair.

Russell Dean looked at his watch. "Ten minutes left. Just enough time for us to talk to Charlie."

Myra could look at him all she wanted now. Her fingers were numb beneath her. She wiggled them. Charlie uncrossed his legs, straightened his back.

"We made a decision about your graduation. You ready to hear it?"

"Yeah."

"You are not well enough to go."

Silence. Charlie didn't look down. He looked right at Russell Dean. "No way. It's my graduation."

"I don't care if it's your Academy Award. You are not well enough to go."

"My *parents* said it was okay."

"No. Your parents said you should do whatever we thought was best."

"You know I won't use."

Now Russell Dean leaned forward, slowly, quietly, squarely. "Do I, Charlie?" He wasn't speaking angrily. Counselors rarely did. But there was an undercurrent of pressure in Russell Dean's words, something he was always holding back. A force of restraint that Myra found herself wanting to submit to.

"You broke your word before."

"I didn't use, though."

"You had sex, Charlie."

Russell Dean glanced at Myra. She swore he did.

"And we had a contract. You. And me."

Myra felt something bite her beneath her ribs, in her throat, in the blades of her shoulders. Was Charlie embarrassed because Myra was there? Did he love her enough to feel like he needed to explain? She had never asked Charlie who that had been—she was afraid he might leave her if she did. This is how weak she was. And weakness was what Small Group revealed. Weakness, fear, desperation. And if anyone looked at her they would see it because group yanked the cover off everyone, even the ones who didn't speak.

"You really think we're going to let you out again?"

Charlie's face was deep red, his mouth tight with rage. Tears welled. He blinked.

"This is bullshit," said Victor. His words slurred.

"You think so?" Russell Dean glared at him. "You thinking keeping an addict from using is *bullshit*?"

He pointed to his own chest.

"You hear that?" Russell Dean looked around the circle. "Anyone hear that?"

"It's the bullshit radar," said Bryan with the weird stubble, drug of choice rush. What was that, anyway?

"That's right. Guess what it's saying, Charlie?" Russell Dean began to growl—a low and careful sound that reminded Myra of a heavy, squeaking door. "*Grrrrrrrrrrrrrrrr.*" He growled again, tapped his chest so hard that Myra could hear a thunk. "This is the bullshit radar. And it's saying, *Grrrrrrrrrrrrrrrr.*" Russell leaned back again and looked into the center, placed his hands on the arms of his chair like a king.

"When you want to tell us about what's really going on, Charlie, you let us know." Russell Dean paused and then stood. They all followed, held hands, and said the Serenity Prayer.

God, grant me the serenity

To accept the things I cannot change

Courage to change the things I can

And the wisdom to know the difference.

Myra said it every time now, sometimes fervently, sometimes continuing the prayer in her mind after it was over. She pictured God hearing her, a man in the sky opening his arms.

Charlie kept his mouth closed and his eyes down, hurried out of the room. She wanted to talk to him so badly. To make sure everything was okay. Because what if he didn't come to the bathroom that night? What if Myra went as usual and stood waiting for him, desperate with desire, but Charlie didn't show? What then?

Departure

One hour and twenty minutes until Myra and Charlie would meet at the door to run. Between the end of lunch and Smoke Break, they had five minutes of unmonitored time. Russell Dean and Rachel were in their offices; Grace and Bliss and other techs were at the nurses' station checking vitals, dispensing meds, or updating charts; patients were either waiting there or sitting at tables in the smoke room or reading their *Big Books* in the lounge. Charlie had said that he and Myra should run at twelve-twenty, in the middle of all the dispersions. They would meet at the door to the unit—the same door that Myra and all the others, in pajamas, had been escorted through on their first day. He and Myra would push it open and enter the hallway. Then they would take the elevator to the hospital lobby. From there, Charlie knew where to go. They would borrow a quarter or find one, and then Charlie would call his best friend Jeff to come and get them.

    Myra was in her study carrel, reading "A Perfect Day for Bananafish" for AP English, wishing for Muriel's confidence, for the bright, easy beach that Sybil played on. She wondered what Seymour did with the trees when he was driving and why he shot himself in the head. Why didn't the story go on from there? What about Muriel? What was she supposed to do now?

Hope you're doing well, Myra, Mr. London had written at the top of the page. *Keep reading!* His classroom was a windowless square on the second floor of City High, with chalkboards on three walls and an empty bulletin board on the fourth. The first time he had called her up to his desk after class, he had told her she was a gifted writer.

Thanks, Myra said, trying to picture the wife he so often mentioned—long feathered hair, skirt, pantyhose, clogs. Mr. London smiled and asked her if she would share some of her journal entries with the class. *I don't think so,* she said. But every few weeks he still asked her to do something, to share herself. Would she like to write an essay for a teenage writing contest about the Iowa River? Would she lead a class discussion about a short story of her choice for extra credit? Would she share just one of her journal entries—what about the one on "A Cask of Amontillado," "A Rose for Emily," or "To Build a Fire?" No way. But thanks a lot for asking, she didn't say sarcastically, because your interest in me does not matter. The warmth of adult praise lasted until the moment was over. It did not make people notice her or help Myra become popular or give her the courage to eat her sack lunch in the cafeteria instead of a girls' room stall. Why didn't adults know the limits of their efforts? Why would they complement someone they couldn't really help?

But he had kept encouraging and eventually asked Myra to confide in him. Myra had been watching a Little Hawks basketball practice after school with Nancy, standing outside the new gymnasium at the vending machine, buying candy for both of them. Nancy never had any money, and Keen always gave Myra some if she didn't ask for too much.

"Hi, Myra," said Mr. London.

She turned around.

"How you doing?"

"Fine."

"I'm glad I saw you," he said. He wore a polo shirt tucked into slacks with a thick brown belt between the two, which made his shoulders look rounded.

"You know your grades have dropped?"

His shoulders were hunched anyway, Myra realized, but that belt tightened into his gut made the curve look worse.

"You want to talk about it?" he asked. "I mean, can I help?"

She held a Twix in one hand and a Reese's in the other. She squeezed the Twix, felt that cushion of air between the bars and the wrapper. Mr. London was nice. Super nice. She saw herself open her mouth and tell him. I wanted to die, she didn't say, but now I've stopped thinking about dying and instead I miss people and things that I never had to begin with. She saw them both standing there in the foyer between the old gym and the new gym. Shades of red surrounded them, painted them in—tiles the color of brick, doors the color of fire engines, railings the color of stop signs.

"I… just don't like reading anymore."

Mr. London looked like someone had stolen something from him. Like his stomach hurt.

"Sorry," Myra said, and she walked through the doors of the new gym, the bounces of basketballs vibrating in her temples, the court floor gleaming. What was that—wax? What was it that polished the surfaces of things? She didn't care. She didn't care about anything.

But Myra did care. She didn't understand why Seymour shot himself or Emily poisoned her husband or Fortunato and the man in the wild had to die, but those moments in literary time triggered in her a deep affection for other people, a desire for love, a devotion to the world and all things and her father, even though he had not written to her. She cared so deeply that it made her lonesome. It made her desperate. She would write Mr. London a note. She would write him a note and leave it in her homework, saying she was sorry, that she was doing okay now that she wanted to be sober, that she hadn't meant to hurt his feelings, that she loved reading stories and always had and that this would never change and that stories were the only things in the world that she could walk through without feeling the eyes of everyone else on her and inside her. And she would read one of her journals to the class when she got back. She really would.

"Hi, Myra."

Margaret, the Recreation director, was standing over her carrel. The clock on the wall behind her read eleven-thirty. Fifty minutes to go.

"Hi," Myra said. Margaret was tall and thin, with hair like Farah Fawcett's. They had Recreation with her on Mondays, Wednesdays, and Thursdays. They didn't do a sport every time, which Myra was grateful for. They did cardio rotation in the basement gymnasium of the hospital building or took brisk walks along the Iowa River bike path. On the last walk, Margaret had let Sam with the bleached hair but brown eyebrows, drug of choice pot, carry the boom box from the indoor rec room. As they walked up the spiraled incline to the footbridge, Huey Lewis' "I Want a New Drug" came on. Sam turned it up. Everyone sang.

"Turn it off!" Margaret called from the front of the line without turning around, her head to the side, her hair feathered all the way to the ends, below her shoulders.

Sam didn't. They all kept singing.

"I said turn it off!"

"No way!" he said.

Margaret halted and therefore stopped the line; like a scene from *Three's Company*, patients bumped into each other as she marched back to Sam. Her beautiful hair that Myra would never pull out if it were hers—no way—flopped in rhythm against her shoulders. She might not have been wearing a bra. She was so thin she didn't need one.

As traffic sped below them, Margaret took the boom box from him and turned it off.

"No way," Sam said again.

"It's not okay," Margaret said.

"It's a love song!" Sam said.

"It's making you think about using, isn't it?"

They all stood in silence. All of them outdoors together felt strange, as if they were an oddity, like furniture on a lawn. The song wasn't making Myra think about using. She'd never done any drugs. She had only images of drugs from TV and stories of pot from Nancy, who had stopped liking it after she smoked some while she was drunk and threw up in Cooper's motorcycle helmet.

"This is not a healthy song for you right now." Her favorite words were healthy, being healthy, having good health, getting healthy. This is what treatment can bring you, she always said. Health is what we're shooting for. Health and peace.

"You got a letter today, Myra," Margaret whispered, placing it beside Myra's notebook. "I didn't want you to have to wait." She smiled and left, her slacks swishing around her skinny legs.

It was from Nancy. One page on thick-lined notebook paper with spiral fringe, the letters round and looped.

Hey Girl!

    How are you? I'm fine. I wish you were here so I could tell you about Cooper! He is such a --------------------. My mom says we are going to move to a new house soon because our neighbor is a jerk. Yay! I went to the Rez with Cindy yesterday and got sunburned soooo bad! Anyway, Cindy says to tell you hi. Cooper too.

Write me back!

Love, Nancy   XOXOXOXO

Myra read it three times, four times, five times, until patients in other carrels stacked their schoolwork and moved their chairs against the wall to make room for the lunch tables. Myra folded up the letter and put it in her back pocket and looked over at the door, where she would meet Charlie. She felt herself warm, glowing like a beacon. Everything felt wonderful. Everything felt fine. Everything had always been fine—she just hadn't known it until now. What was she even doing here? Myra felt what she thought was a wave of serenity spread through her chest, settle her fluttering stomach. She thought she might soar with the airiness of it all, with the peace.

And soon Charlie would be with her.

**

Twelve-fifteen. Lunch was over, tables folded up.

Myra was sitting in a chair in the lounge, her feet up on the windowsill. The sun was shining on the Des Moines River as she pretended to read "How it Works," a key chapter from the *Alcoholics Anonymous Big Book*:

First of all, we had to quit playing God. It didn't work. Next, we decided that hereafter in this drama of life, God was going to be our Director. He is the Principal; we are His agents. He is the Father, and we are His children…

We had a new Employer. Being all powerful, He provided what we needed, if we kept close to Him and performed His work well. Established on such a footing we became less and less interested in ourselves, our little plans and designs.

Twelve-nineteen. Were they actually going to do this? Myra closed her *Big Book* and put it on the seat of her chair. Should she casually walk toward the door, as if she were just walking toward the door? Of course she should. The nurses were up at their station. Where was Charlie? But they had planned this. They would stay in Jeff's basement, probably—his parents never went down there. But if that wouldn't keep them from being found, Charlie would think of something else. They would spend the night somewhere and return before noon the next day.

It was happening. It would happen. It was time and everything was fine. She walked through the lounge as if she were going somewhere she understood. Her face and neck were tingling, burning. She coiled hair around her ring finger. This was her favorite one, actually, so different from the index finger. So unexpected and fleshy.

"Hi, Myra."

Jen wore tight, ripped jeans, penny loafers, a pink polo. Her hair was sprayed back into a ponytail.

"Hey, Jen."

"You're holding your hair," she said. "That's not okay."

Myra let it go. "Thanks."

"You're talking more in group. I think you've been doing so great."

"Oh. Yeah."

Behind Jen, in the hallway, Charlie waited at the door, staring at Myra.

"What you said to Abbey and everything," Jen said. Jen had been confronting Abbey often, Abbey who never seemed weak or indecisive, who did not budge, her stance unyielding and her affect stoic and her arms eternally crossed and her gaze not ever on the floor but right at whoever challenged her—usually Jen—as if to say, *Go ahead.*

"You think this is funny?" Jen had said in group. "We're telling you how sick we are of your attitude, and you think it's funny? We're *scared* for you," Jen said. "Don't you understand?" Grin continued.

Jen started to cry. "I can't believe you're doing this to yourself! I'm trying to help you!"

"Tell her how you feel, Jen," said Rachel.

"Hurt," said Jen. "Angry. Hurt."

Grin, grin, grin.

"Why are you so, like, hateful?" Myra asked.

Everyone, including Abbey, looked at Myra, who had never confronted anyone before.

"Do you have to be that way all the time?" Myra asked.

Abbey's grin shrunk back to scowl. She reset her crossed arms.

Charlie was waiting. The clock read twelve twenty-two. Should she walk away? Leave Jen standing there? Wouldn't she hurt Jen's feelings? A lot? She should say something to her—Myra knew this, but the words did not emerge. She had to go. Myra smiled at Jen with a strange, closed mouth. She walked past her and then through the door with Charlie. Into The Outs.

Freedom

Nancy was sixteen the first time her mother had spent the night away. She sat Nancy down in the front room and gave her ten dollars.

"You're so mature," she said. "You'll be okay on your own."

Nancy held the money in her hand. She was dressed in her black jeans and an Esprit sweater, hair curled but makeup not yet finished.

"Mack doesn't like teenagers," her mother said. "He isn't ready to spend a lot of time with you yet."

"You're not coming home?" Her feet were bare against the carpet.

"Not until tomorrow after work. Mack is getting impatient." She stood up, her skirt ironed and crisp, her hair long with feathered bangs. She wore a new blazer to cover the ketchup stain on her blouse, a stain Nancy had tried to help her get out years before. Bleach didn't even work. "It won't be regular, I promise. But Lucy might drop in."

Lucy was Nancy's older sister, living with her douchebag boyfriend. Mack was also a douchebag boyfriend. Skinny, weird, stoic. When Nancy thought of him with her mom, like physically, she cringed. But Mack had money and a super-nice car. He bought jewelry and new clothes for her mother, gave Nancy a leather jacket, some awesome boots.

"It'll be good practice for the real world," her mother said, walking out the front door of their duplex. Butch, on his chain in the front yard, lifted his head and peered in. "And that's only a couple years away. Plenty of food in the fridge. See you tomorrow! You have Mack's number for emergencies only, okay?"

And then her mother had just… stayed away. She came home every few days to unpack groceries and clean up a little and get new sets of clothes. Sometimes she made Hamburger Helper or spaghetti with Ragu for her and Nancy to share. She called Nancy every night at seven. Sometimes Nancy picked up. Sometimes she was with Cooper. Sometimes she wasn't there.

Cooper started sleeping over more often. After school he'd bring Dave and Mark over to make toast and watch Cinemax. He wanted to have parties.

"My mom wouldn't like that," she said, pretending to believe her mother might care. "No way. Not happening."

"Come on, Nance," said Cooper. He reached his hand beneath her shirt and rubbed her stomach. They were watching TV in her basement on the waterbed. Cooper had freckles, a turned-up nose, and a baseball cap.

"You guys will get drunk and trash my house," she said. She had started cleaning more, wiping off old coatings of grease in the kitchen, folding her laundry instead of letting it pile on the floor. "So no." Nancy didn't drink very much. Sometimes with Myra on Fridays, but that was it. She liked to be in control.

Cooper kissed her neck, unsnapped her jeans. She pushed his hand away, reached for her Dr. Pepper. "You can have parties at Dave's, like always. Not here." Dave's parents didn't care, and they had a bigger house.

Nancy started to turn schoolwork in on time. Started making sure she was there for class, called Cooper to come pick her up early in the mornings so she would be in homeroom on time. Started asking her mother for money.

"Mack's not a bank," her mother would say. Nancy heard a TV in the background.

"He stole you from me," Nancy said. "You know he did. It's the least he could do."

Next day, some cash in an envelope in the mail slot. Nancy set it aside for beauty school.

She loved hair. She could do hair and makeup all day. She wanted to do Cindy Lauper because that woman was so pretty but she looked like shit, like a crazy person trying to be famous.

She practiced on Myra, but Myra only wanted to keep makeup on if she'd been drinking beer. When Myra drank, she would do anything. She could be unpredictable. Nancy needed to watch her, keep an eye on things. She understood now that she liked being in charge, having control, making sure everyone was okay.

Performance Part 1

The quarter was on the curb as if someone had left it for them, clean and shiny in the shadow of a parking ramp, the sun lost in all the gray—the four-lane street, the concrete buildings, the sidewalk. Myra was familiar with nothing here in the capital of Iowa—no street names, parks, schools, intersections. She was dependent on Charlie, and they had not been holding hands, as she had envisioned they would—not since they left the unit and then the hospital building, not when they walked down the bike path along the river, not when they crossed a bridge and entered this downtown space. Was it downtown? Where were they? Charlie maintained a steady forward gaze and a pace so fast that Myra was nearly jogging to claim her place beside him. There was no kiss, no display of love to mark the start of their journey.

"We can't let any cops see us," Charlie said. Clothing store on the right, street on the left. Big hotel with circular drive ahead. "They called them as soon as they knew we were gone. And we're not in school. A cop stops us, we're dead."

Myra thought she might stop Charlie and kiss him. Take the initiative and do what she felt. But then she saw the quarter.

"Charlie." She pointed.

"Awesome!" He picked it up. "There's a phone booth around the corner, I'm pretty sure."

A blue stripe of TELEPHONE bordered the top edge, its glass walls hazy and smeared with fingerprints. The folding door squeaked. Charlie left it open.

"I'm calling Jeff. Look out for cops." He pushed the quarter into the slot.

"What if he's not home?"

"He's home. He has open lunch and then study hall."

"What if his mom answers?" From a parking meter, a man in a suit with a briefcase was staring at them. Myra looked away.

"He has his own line."

Myra grabbed his hand and wrapped her fingers into his. His shirt was green with white buttons below the collar, his hair longer than Myra's and a dark, shiny yellow in the daylight. Myra's hair was growing in, but the patches were still obvious enough for her to use bobby pins in the back, underneath, to hide all the uneven growth. But her bangs had been perfect that morning, feathered just enough not to look sprayed in place. Charlie squeezed her hand, hard, and smiled at her as he spoke into the receiver. Parked cars lined the curb behind him, their colors muted in the shadow of the parking ramp.

***

Jeff's basement was padded in dark blue carpet. Beanbags circled the television, a giant square of wood framing with fake drawers down one side and a 26-inch screen. MTV showed Michael Jackson without sound. They could stay down here, Jeff said, but they needed to be out of the house between six and ten, when his parents got home from the hospital where they worked. If they were quiet when they woke up it should be fine because his parents never came down here in the mornings. Jeff handed Charlie a key. He had pimples, lots of them, and hair in a loose ponytail that hung to his shoulder blades.

"Thanks, man," Charlie said. He put his arm around Myra. They were sitting on the basement couch, which was covered in a plaid fabric so scratchy that Myra could feel it through her jeans. Was it burlap? Wool? It reminded her of fiberglass, like the horse-swings in the City Park playground in Iowa City that had sometimes left splinters in Myra's thighs as a child. Jeff told them to eat whatever they wanted and that he'd be home from school before they had to leave. As soon as he closed the door at the top of the basement stairs and locked it behind him, Charlie put his hand on Myra's chin and turned her face toward his, just like a lover on *General Hospital*, and their mouths opened to one another and he squeezed Myra's breasts and then reached up her shirt.

She didn't know what to do except let herself experience whatever he wanted. He unsnapped and unzipped her pants and Myra disappeared into the waves of euphoria in her gut, her vagina, her hips. He slid his fingers beneath the waistband of her underwear and moved his knuckles gently across her stomach, then, like always, inserted one finger inside her. Was it gross to gasp or moan or grunt? She felt a rush that was both quick and slow, then a release, a lift in her hips. She stifled the moan for fear of revealing herself, of pleasure being discovered. His fingers—two now—reached further. Myra exhaled against his cheek and then kissed him again, pulled him closer to her but tried to cover her panting. She opened her eyes mid-kiss—his were slitted closed and his cheeks moved like gears, like the inner-workings of a clock or a motor.

She moved with him on the couch, her head pressed into the armrest, the abrasive cover matting her hair, crunching it up. She had come. She must have. Did he know? Did he care? She saw his nose as if for the first time. His nose was longer than she had realized before, the light from the basement windows just enough to see the hourglass shape of his nostrils, a faint freckle on the outer curve of that thick skin. Almost like cartilage but not stiff enough, probably. What did she know, anyway? Was it cartilage or wasn't it?

Charlie moved off of her and sat up.

"We don't have a condom," he said, sitting up at Myra's feet. "Shit. We don't have a condom."

Neither had Nancy and Cooper. Myra had always known they had sex—Nancy said every day sometimes—but Myra never asked about birth control. Until Nancy told her she was pregnant, Myra always pictured them together on Nancy's bed, having sex atop all her dirty clothes, or on her basement floor, the carpeting thick and wall-to-wall.

"Will you go with me?" Nancy asked. They were in the sweats and T-shirts they had slept in the night before, eating Ruffles and Dr. Pepper for breakfast in Nancy's waterbed in her basement. They were both hung over—Cooper had brought them wine coolers and after he left to go to a party they had drunk all of them, smoking cigarettes like adults right there in Nancy's house. Her mother was never home, and she didn't care anyway. They had sat on the deck between two broken chaise lounges and took turns getting up to rewind "Hard Habit to Break" and "You're the Inspiration," sang the words in lush, slurred misery, blew smoke into the night sky, and flicked butts onto the lawn. Nancy had set out all her makeup and put some on Myra—a layer of foundation, then glittery blush. To make Myra's eyes look big, she brushed a bold stripe of wet black on that delicate strip of skin above the lower lashes that started at the tear duct. Myra hoped her eyes would look like Erica Kane's. How eyes were supposed to look.

How did you remove makeup from such a tender place? Myra had slept in it and now her right eye burned.

"Have you told Cooper?" Myra asked.

"He wouldn't go." She drank from the 2-liter bottle of Dr. Pepper (all the glasses had been dirty) and handed it to Myra.

"Yes he would."

"It might not be his anyway." An old purple comforter cushioned them all around. "Shit." She started to cry.

"Oh my God, Nancy."

Nancy wiped her nose with her fingers and looked at the 9-inch television that sat on the dresser below the window.

"Whose is it?"

"Maybe Dave's."

On MTV, Whitney Houston wore a blue-purple dress with a V down the back and an upside-down V up the bottom and matching evening gloves over her long, slender arms. It was her first video.

"She is so pretty," Nancy said. She ate another chip. "Will you go with me?"

"Yeah." Myra smiled gently. "When is it?"

"Next Friday after school. Cooper thinks I'll be at your house."

"I'll drive you."

But Myra still didn't care about birth control. She put the need away like a book she didn't want to read. Charlie sat at Myra's feet, the stairs behind him painted white, leading up to the kitchen. She lay there in her unzipped jeans, her bra unhooked and pushed up to her collar bones along with her shirt. She felt her breasts in the open air, her nipples stiff with basement chill. She wanted him to look at her semi-nakedness, gaze at her, reach for her in the light of day because he could not help himself.

"I'm going to look in Jeff's room." He went up the stairs. Myra blew on her nipples and touched them, circled her areola with her fingertips, rubbed the tiny bumps. Tightened her vagina. She heard his footsteps above her, looked at the ceiling, put her hand on her stomach. The fabric pressing into her back made her itch. Who would put this on furniture? She was freezing—the air conditioning seemed to blow through the vents nonstop—so she sat up and pulled her shirt down and reached back to hook her bra but then sat back into the couch and left it, left her pants unzipped too, just in case Charlie wanted to keep going. So she should lay there like a lifeless doll the whole time he was upstairs? Why was being eager so distasteful? What was wrong with being honest? She might ruin it, that's what. And what if she ruined this chance she'd been given? Myra wanted so much to talk to him. But if she did, what would she say? *Charlie, are you mad at me? Did I do something?* Gross. *Charlie, I'm so afraid, I love you so much, do you think about me as much as I think about you?* Grosser. What if she restricted her comments to the moment they were in? Instead of telling him all the bigger truths that meant she was desperate, what if she told him the little truths? The day-to-day desperates. Like I statements. *Charlie, I'm feeling insecure, and I'm not sure if you really care about me.*

Totally disgusting.

Myra did not think she would get pregnant: she had thought about it a few times with Chad Norris and felt her brain perform an action, a flicking away. When she thought of getting pregnant by Charlie, she was sure she loved him. Was that so bad? To want him that much? Why was she ashamed for wanting such a thing? Maybe she would have the baby. Maybe they would get married. Charlie would have to commit to her, or at least he would have to be there during the abortion. He would insist. She pictured herself in the same office she had taken Nancy, Charlie in the waiting room with the stiff brown folding chairs while she went back.

When it was done, Nancy came through the door to the waiting area fast and kept walking, barely scanning the room for Myra. Her eyes were misty, her mascara and eyeliner smudged. She looked like she wanted to run for help, find an antidote, grab the buoy. Myra hiked their purses over her shoulder and followed her out the front door, into the sun of Clinton Street. Behind them, on either side of the Iowa River, the university sprawled around the old capitol dome, pristine buildings and enclaves and walkways and history. A Cambus roared by.

"I have a lot of pads. I'll bleed for a few days. I don't know what I'll tell Cooper."

"That you're sick. I'll tell him for you."

"He'll want to anyway."

"You could stay at my house. Tomorrow, too. My dad will be there, but we can just stay in my room and watch TV."

Nancy nodded. "I'd tell my mom where I'll be, but she won't care anyway."

Myra's Nova had not started that morning; Nancy had taken the bus to Myra's house, since she lived close to downtown, and then they had walked to the clinic. Nancy took her purse from Myra and hooked it over her shoulder. It was six blocks to Myra's house. Nancy looked drugged, spaced out, glazed over.

"Want to get a cherry Coke at Pearson's?" Myra asked. They walked slowly past the gas station. Two girls on Clinton Street on a spring afternoon.

***

She heard Charlie coming down the stairs. What if she told him she didn't care about birth control? What if he knew? Would he still like her, or would he think she was desperate?

Performance Part 2

It was a sweet slippery pain, smooth and strong and commanding. Myra sucked air and held her arms around Charlie's shoulders and saw in the dimmed floodlights the trees bowing way over their heads, and, as usual, she could not identify them. Cars zoomed on a highway in the distance. The grass on the golf course was so short she couldn't even feel it pressing into her back through the thin sheet they had taken from Jeff's. The ground was hard. A warm breeze blew on her neck. It was June, after all, June in Iowa, and the air was not yet sopping wet, but it was hot, and mosquitoes bit her legs as she held them open to Charlie's thrusts and then pulled them in to cradle his torso. She was looking at the trees without focus, layers of green in all the leaves.

***

On their way to the gas station for a condom, he had held her hand. They walked along a strip of restaurants and gas stations and a Kmart and Kmart-like stores and soccer fields, but the strip had no sidewalk, so they'd walked on the hard dirt of the shoulder or across various parking lots. It was getting dark, Charlie had said, so he doubted anyone would really notice them. People walked this strip all the time. There was no need to worry.

A semi boomed past them. Then another.

"So I've had sex with four other people," Charlie said.

"Were they your girlfriends?" Their hands were starting to sweat together, palms warming.

Charlie shook his head. "Just friends and stuff. How many people have you had sex with?"

"One," Myra said. She decided to say something that would make her appear to be a different kind of person than she was. "He was a dick."

Charlie laughed. "I won't be a dick. Don't worry."

They reached the gas station, and she stood outside the glass door while Charlie went to the men's room to buy a condom from the machine. It was a barren place, with one narrow refrigerator of beer and pop, a wire rack of candy resting on the counter. The attendant wore a stained brown uniform. He was filthy. Myra was glad he barely looked at them. Out the window behind him, an orange Beetle Bug stood in the air on a hydraulic lift, puddles of oil on the gravel beneath.

"Got one!" Charlie grabbed her hand and led her back down the strip. It was darker now. Cars were using headlights through the gray.

***

Charlie was finished. He touched her cheek. "You okay?"

Myra smiled. "Yeah."

Charlie pulled himself out of her, peeled off the condom, and flung it into the trees.

"Let's be naked!"

He stood up. They were hidden in a cove, masked by trees, beside a tiny pond and a sand trap. They could hear mosquitoes all around them but for some reason Myra wasn't feeling bites anymore. Fluid came out of her in folds, soaking the sheet.

Charlie jumped along the edge of the pond as if he had a pogo stick. "I love being naked!"

Myra wanted to wipe herself with the sheet but felt it would appear disgusting. She pulled up her underwear, wincing, then her jeans, and she saw in her back pocket Nancy's letter from that morning, a corner of the white paper poking up. Nancy. Nancy would love this story. When Myra got out, she would tell Nancy everything.

Everything except the part where they returned to Jeff's and put cushions on the floor to sleep on and sat in front of the television and started making out, slowly removing clothes. Charlie didn't mention a condom and of course Myra didn't either. She wondered if, their first time, the condom had been a sort of icebreaker, and if now they wouldn't use one anymore. She was hungry, tired, sore. She doubted very much that Charlie's penis was sore, swollen, or sticky. She doubted that he felt repulsed when he had to pull on the same underwear.

She didn't want to do it again. She wanted to go to sleep.

"You want to do it doggie style?" Charlie asked, grinning.

"What's that?" she asked.

"You don't know what doggie style is?" Charlie got a cigarette from the pocket of his jeans and lit it and offered one to Myra. She took it and shook her head.

He moved from the cushions, the TV blinking behind him, the only light in the room. She could almost see his shadow on the carpet when he got on his hands and knees. He thrust his hips several times, his penis and testicles bouncing along with him, and then he held the position. He looked at Myra, his eyebrows up and his cigarette hanging from his mouth.

Myra shook her head so quickly she didn't realize it—it felt almost like a tremor. She had no idea what his demonstration meant. Where was she supposed to be if he was on his hands and knees?

"No."

"Okay." Charlie lay beside her and held her hand, blew smoke at the ceiling, and Myra rubbed his fingers with her thumb, smooth compressions over the ridges in his knuckles.

***

In Myra's dreams, her mother was in other women's bodies. She was Nancy's mom. She was the bartender at the Ramada. She was Kim Carnes. She was Mrs. O'Hara, her fifth-grade teacher. Now her mother became Mrs. Hunsicker, the City High P.E. teacher who watched Myra in the locker room to make sure she showered. Mrs. Hunsicker watched all the girls but especially Myra because she knew how Myra despised P.E. Instead of participating in any stupid thing they were forced to do that made Myra feel weak and powerless and frantic to be someplace else, Myra stood with her arms crossed tight while a softball, or soccer ball, or volleyball, or basketball sped past her. Because how was she supposed to stand? As if she were really going to catch something? What should she do with her arms? What position could she possibly assume that didn't make her feel like an engorged zit on a clear face? Why did she have to be there at all, in the center of everything while no one noticed her? A boy almost always covered for her anyway—Stanley Sminken the wrestler, Elvin Barry who smelled, Tommy Christianson who sold pot—they were the saviors of all the teens who hated P.E.

When it ended, Myra walked fast to the locker room, dropped her clothes, and wrapped her torso in one of their scratchy towels, felt her butt hanging out and slouched her shoulders to try and get the towel to hang lower. None of the girls wanted anyone to see them naked. But Myra was curious and ashamed for being curious, and as she dreamed the desire and the knowledge were a force that rose in her throat and made her want to speak, to yell for help, to prevent a tragedy, an uncovering. She inhaled the steam, felt the mist on her toes from the foot spray-pump you stepped on as you walked into the shower and again as you walked out. And when Myra did walk out, there was Mrs. Hunsicker, unwarm and strange with weird, frog-like lips, checking Myra's shoulders to see if they were wet. Reaching over and touching the top of her head.

"Your hair is dry," said Mrs. Hunsicker, in her mother's voice. The locker room bubbled with conversation from the other girls. Concrete blocks and tile painted dark red with white stripes. The school colors.

"I took a shower."

"Go on." She put her hands on Myra's shoulders, turned her around. "I'll be waiting right here."

Mom, Myra cried. Her eyes opened and she could not move. She blinked. The clock ticked. She sat up. Charlie, who was asleep, had left the television on without sound: a white hand reached up from the diner table in "Take on Me," the video by a-ha. She tried to decide if the girl in the video was pretty or not, then looked down at Charlie. She had never seen a boy asleep before. She had never slept beside a boy before. Charlie was still naked, his body covered with a sheet. His nose was still big. In the light of the television, his acne marks made him look weathered, as if he were older, a pioneer tired from a day of clearing prairie to build a log cabin. Myra remembered from a history class that the tallgrass prairie had grown over seven feet high. If cattle went missing, farmers had to stand on the backs of their horses to spot them.

Myra lay back down and pulled the Iowa State blanket over her chest. The space between her breasts was damp with sweat, sorrow, longing, with the power of her mother's dead voice and the earth that Myra knew so little about. Places, plants, textures, origins. The vagueness was what held.

***

Myra and Charlie walked into the hospital at eleven o'clock in the morning, the lobby empty except for the stiff furniture, plastic chairs with metal legs, a glassed-in wall of information desks. Charlie pushed the elevator button, his face stiff with fear and his finger trembling just a little. When they got to the unit, it would be goodbye. Didn't Charlie realize this? Would he hold her hand? Put his arm around her? They stepped into the elevator; he pushed 4. The doors closed.

"I am so fucking dead," Charlie said.

"Come here," Myra said, reaching her hand toward him. "Quick."

"Not now."

The doors parted. And there stood Russell Dean, as if he had been waiting for them, sent from above, his clipboard and files tucked under one arm. Beside him was Billy, who was graduating that day, and so with Billy were his mother, father, and little sister. Myra became aware of her tangled and fuzzed hair, the dirt smudged all over her legs, the layers of transparent grime on her teeth, the cavernous growls in her stomach that grew louder as Billy's family stared at her and Charlie for the longest few seconds in the history of time.

Billy looked a little crushed. When people ran, they let everyone down. They broke trust. They damaged the Community. Billy's parents looked confused. His sister, five years old, sucked on a lollipop and held her mother's hand.

"Why, it's Myra and Charlie!" Russell Dean said, his face spreading into the grin, the one that knew everything. "So nice to see you!" He gestured to Billy and his family to enter the elevator while Myra and Charlie walked out of it. They looked up at Russell Dean as he put his hands fiercely on their backs.

"March your asses down to the nurses' station. We'll chat later over tea."

They walked. "Shit," Charlie said. "Shit. Shit. Shit."

Way down the hall were Bliss and Grace, standing at the counter, writing in charts. In a security mirror above them, Myra saw tiny versions of herself and Charlie, the convex curve pushing them far apart, much further than they really were.

Damage

Grace would not let her take a shower. After Recreation, she said. On the weekends, when the main counselors were off and patients didn't have Small Group in the morning and afternoon, they went to the rec room on the floor below the unit. A few of them looked out the large observation windows over the Iowa River below or sat with their *Big Books* and worked on their assignments, legal pads or spirals in their laps. Other patients played the one mixed tape they had over and over on the boom box. "Birthday," "Leroy Brown," "Peace Train," "Hotel California." They sang as loud as they could, afternoon sun shining across the foosball table as they danced.

But today was Wednesday, and it was time for Recreation, and everyone would play softball in the diamond across the street.

"You can shower afterward," Grace said. Myra sat on the exam table in the tiny nurses' office behind their station while Grace took her blood pressure and checked her eyes and nose and throat, checked her reflexes, and took her temperature. "Like everyone else. The last thing you get right now is special treatment. Did you use?"

"No." Out the tiny rectangle of a window was rooftop that looked like a giant shingle.

"We'll see." She handed Myra a urine cup and opened the door, led her through the patients who were waiting at the counter for their mid-day meds. Myra met their eyes. The boys smiled. The girls didn't.

Myra sat down and tried to pee. She had been with Charlie. That was what she had wanted. And she wanted to be with him every day for the rest of her life. She searched for the elation but instead felt her urine, burning out as if through a pinhole in a balloon. Her guts felt swollen, her vaginal skin tender and sore.

Grace told Myra to go straight to lunch.

"Can I change clothes?"

"What do you think?"

Bliss made her sit alone at one end of a mostly empty table.

"You're on No Contact," Bliss said calmly. Her elbows were skeletal. She stood over Myra and watched her sit down with her tray. Reubens! It was Rueben day, everyone's favorite. Chocolate cake for dessert. Myra was starving. "That means eye contact, too."

But when Bliss wasn't looking, Abbey waved. Jen pretended Myra wasn't there. Charlie sat across the room, also eating alone, not looking at her or trying to. One signal. One sign from him and she'd do whatever he wanted. Just like with Chad Norris. Just like with Mark. She felt the pattern of her behavior, her history, etching itself in.

She was tired. She had barely slept. The plaid Izod she had worn since yesterday looked like someone had run it over.

After lunch, they all went to their rooms and changed into shorts and T-shirts for softball. Myra's legs were red with mosquito bites. She had scratched the ones around her ankles until a few of them bled, and she had swatches of dirt on her calves and a giant swirl of it on her thigh that she had noticed in the mirror just as Margaret opened the door to Myra's room.

"Let's go."

"I didn't use," Myra said. "I promise." Her inner thigh muscles—what were they called?—hurt. Her quads hurt. Her vagina hurt. Her forearms were sore. She was thirsty after that Rueben.

"Do you know what you've done?"

"I called my dad. I didn't use."

"Jen was sobbing last night. She and Victor were worried sick. Billy was so mad he didn't eat. All his hard work. And Charlie—I can't even talk about him. He wasn't here for Billy's last Community. You know that?"

"I'm sorry," Myra said.

"You'll have plenty of people to say that to. And after softball, it's five days of pajamas for both of you."

"Why?"

"So you know how sick you are."

Myra started in the outfield, on second base. The bright sun made her squint. Her legs looked like they were not hers, her feet too far from her head. She smiled, laughed a little, cheered for whoever was at bat, hated the baseball glove that smelled like feet, cracked and rough on her palm. She felt an empty sense of euphoria and a violent sense of embarrassment, the daylight around her a backdrop to her view of herself.

"Hi, Myra."

Myra turned around to see Mitch with the doughy face, drug of choice Budweiser, standing right behind her. He had moved forward from the outfield.

"What happened to your legs?" He had a deep, loud voice. He was seventeen, a senior from Ames, a football player, a prom king. His skin was pasty, his stomach beer-full but not fat, his hair feathered above and below his ears. This was the first time Myra had seen him in anything except hospital pajamas. He was on Day Six.

"Mosquitoes," Myra said. "Charlie has them, too." Myra watched as he looked from her ankles to her face. Up and down. Twice. She felt flattered and repulsed, thrilled and sickened. She'd felt these oxymorons before; in eighth grade during study hall, she'd gotten a note from two popular boys. A stick figure of her with a large arrow pointing to her crotch: "Does this go with your butt and tits?" When she got up to throw it away, they watched her walk from her desk to the trash bin and back. She had felt that stare many times. Even when no boys were staring at her, she felt like they were—a constant pull, an urgency.

He grinned. "Where did you go?"

Should she tell him anything? Was he somehow trying to be her friend? He was standing too close. Across the field, Charlie stood in line to bat with the other team, talking, violating No Contact. She supposed she just had, too. Was Charlie talking about her? Would he tell them how it felt to have sex with Myra? Would he laugh at her? Would he tell them that she was beautiful? How did boys talk to each other about girls? Why didn't she know? What should she do right at this moment to keep from crying?

She looked right into Mitch's tiny eyes.

"Paris."

Mitch laughed as Jen hit the ball—it rolled right to Myra. She tried to scoop it up but her glove slipped off; when she pulled it back on and stood, Mitch threw the ball to first base. If there was anything Myra hated more than softball, she couldn't think what it was. She crossed her arms, rolled her eyes, imagined setting her glove on fire. The sun burned her back; her T-shirt was so hot against her shoulders she wondered if it was scalding her skin.

Tina was catcher. Margaret was umpire. Charlie was up to bat. He was not an athlete. He dropped acid and listened to Frank

Zappa and smoked pot and cigarettes. And he hated jocks—he had told her so. But he had confidence, as if he had potential and knew it. Myra had never seen a girl who wasn't in sports have this kind of comfort with them. She wondered if the confidence came before the sport, and she wondered why so many girls didn't have any; she wasn't the only one who stood like a statue in the midst of a game and waited for it to end. But Charlie, despite his detachment from sports, could make baskets, could catch a ball. So when he went up to home plate, bat in hand, Mitch and all the others on Myra's team backed up. Myra stayed where she was. She put her weight on one foot and let her other hip rest out. Sweat dripped down her back.

"What base you going to get to, Charlie?" Mitch called.

The metaphor. It almost made Myra's knees buckle. Took the moisture from her mouth. Please, God, no.

Bryan threw the pitch. Charlie missed.

"Strike one!" called Margaret. It was hot and breezeless.

Bryan pitched again.

"Strike two!"

Myra put her weight on her other leg. Held her breath.

"Come on!" Mitch called. "You going to score another home run, Charlie?"

The boys whooped and laughed. The girls did, too; a few of them whispered to each other. Would Margaret do anything? Say something to them? Myra tried to stay still, like the trunk of an ancient tree, unaffected by her environment, stoic. Jen was on Myra's team, playing first base, hair sprayed back so hard that not one strand frizzed up. She didn't look at Myra, but she didn't laugh either. Myra would ignore them. But how? Look away? Toward what? Act as if she didn't care? How would she do that since she did? Or should she drop her glove and cry? Yell? Rise above it like a better person? Every clichéd instruction would fail her if she tried.

"That's enough, everyone!" Margaret called.

God, please take these feelings from me. I turn them over to you. I turn everything over to you. Wasn't this the answer? Step Three: Turned our will and our lives over to the care of God as we understood Him. Please take my shame away. Please help me. She tried to remember the official third step prayer from the *Big Book* but couldn't.

Sam threw the pitch, and while it was in the air Myra knew what was going to happen and realized what she should do: laugh, clap, shrug it off. Myra pretended to be ready to catch the ball if anyone threw it to her, spread her legs apart, assumed the stance of an athlete, an identity she would never have. When Charlie hit the home run and laughter burst from the softball field, Myra stood and watched the ball. Charlie ran around the bases; the boys applauded, whistled, celebrated, slapped him a line of high fives. She quickly pulled out a strand of hair and exhaled with the pain and what she assumed had been God's will, soaring over her head.

Anxiety

Mitch had gone to Central Junior High, a small building right in the middle of Iowa City that had closed down probably because the school was a shithole of peeling paint and sagging ceilings and cracking plaster. Mitch had a memory from Central he wanted to bring up in group. It was that month of P.E. when Coach Chambers, as he gave directions to the class on whatever they were doing that day—obstacle course, fitness test, dodge ball—reached down the back of Mitch's shorts and lifted him up by the waistband of his underwear and held him up in the air like a giant rubber spider. The first two times, Mitch kicked like a toddler, which made all the kids laugh harder. But the third time, when the class was spread across the lanes of the track field, Mitch stilled himself, crossed his arms as he hung, suspended, and breathed through it. He lifted his head and smirked before Chambers dropped him into the dirt, and when Chambers turned away Mitch gave him the finger. The kids quieted. He stood up and brushed himself off and pulled his underwear into place. Mitch had won. He had overcome by not fighting.

    Chambers never did it again, but Mitch felt something sink fast into his chest, something that crushed his bones but was also heavy in the air, strange and foreboding. He felt surrounded and tried not to talk because he didn't know what he might say. He might scream; he might whine like a puppy; he might collapse. So he closed his mouth and breathed hard through his nose and listened to whoever was speaking near him, but the mouths of other people seemed stiff and slow and twisted, as if someone had dropped him into a horror movie.

A few years passed, but the thing never went away. When he focused on whatever he was doing—a harness run in football practice, a trig worksheet at his kitchen table, a bong in his best friend's cousin's room—the thing disappeared. But it always came back and either disappeared again or made him afraid, and when the fear settled into people's mouths again, he drowned it out with loud insults. He laughed at zitty freshman. His stupid ugly sister. The fattest girl in school, who could've been pretty underneath if she wasn't a pig. His mom, who nagged his dad for drinking until he went into his shop in the basement and didn't come upstairs after dinner anymore.

Mitch wanted to talk about the thing. And he would have, eventually, because since his mom admitted him to OPP, it was getting harder and harder to forget it was in him, as much a part of his body as an organ or a muscle. Sometimes his heart pounded so hard that he started to sweat, and if he was by himself he would close his eyes and clench his fists or his pillow or his teeth and lie to himself and whisper: *I'm okay, I'm okay, I'm okay*. If he wasn't by himself, he smiled and pretended to hear things over the panic and heard the distant sound of whatever emerged from his mouth—acquiescence, question, insult, objection—as the thing encased him in a bubble of air.

Consequences

Myra sat in her hospital pajamas, legs crossed, robe open with the hem brushing the carpet. She twisted the sash around her wrist; Rachel told her to leave her hands in her lap. It had been two days since she returned, and Myra was still waiting to be confronted, what boys called reamed. She wanted it. But this desire was nothing she could admit to. Patients sat in lines along the hallway floor outside the counselor's offices and said *I hope I'm not up today*, or *Fuck. It's going to be my turn, I know it.* They had to act like they despised the attention because saying you wanted it was disgusting. Repugnant. She wanted to be humiliated? Made to cry in front of everyone, her transgressions held up like an x-ray?

Yes. Because wouldn't all those eyes on her make her feel good? Whenever Myra let her awareness revise itself into feeling or emotion, she became relieved, almost comfortable. She understood herself, discovered calm. Was that serenity?

It was Jen's turn again. She had her legal pad open on her lap, with fourteen defects of character to share and explain.

"That's too many," Rachel said. "For now, pick three."

"But I have all of them. Every single one." Jen tapped on the open page with her index finger. "Right here. I do them all. I can prove it." She had begged to jump way ahead to Step Six, where you listed your character defects.

"I think three is reasonable. I know I said okay to this, but you're going through the Steps too quickly."

"But I need to share all of them."

"I don't want you to write your fourth step inventory with so much rehearsal. What if you wrote it with these defects in mind, and left out other things that might be important to your recovery?"

"Oh."

"The steps are in order for a reason." Rachel smiled.

"I don't know how to pick only three."

"Which three are the worst?" Tina asked.

"Which ones do you hate the most?" Theresa asked.

"I hate them all."

They weren't going to talk to Myra. They weren't going to confront her at all. Tears welled up.

"Okay." Jen looked down, flipped the pad over, skimmed it. "Resentment, envy, and perfectionism."

Why wasn't Myra like Abbey, who clearly obviously truly hated every minute of being confronted, hated being in the center? When Abbey refused to talk, or share, or do an assignment, it was because she was angry, but her anger fueled self-respect. She would do what she felt and you would have to put up with it. Lisa was different. She didn't refuse to do anything, but she didn't want attention. She was shy, but she wore shyness like a tailored gown, like Christie Brinkley. And since Myra knew all that Lisa had been through—heroin addiction, homelessness—she thought her shyness was protective, and it struck Myra as sweet. Tender. Something to put on a pedestal. Abbey's anger was protective, too—but it was hostile. People other than Myra might reject someone like Abbey, fear being loved by girls like her. But Myra liked the angry ones and wished she were angry, too. Wished she could wear it like armor. Wished she were not herself.

"Thanks, Jen," Rachel said when Jen had finished. Rachel gazed into the center of the circle like a witch. Myra started to cry.

"Abbey, would you pass Myra the Kleenex, please? And let's go around and tell Myra how her run made us feel."

"Can I say something?" Myra asked.

"Not yet," said Rachel. "You need to hear from the group. Jen, why don't you start?"

"You hurt me so much—"

"Use I."

"Right. Okay. Um, I feel so hurt by what you did. I feel betrayed. Like you were just pretending to be into the program."

"Me, too," said Tina. "Your actions speak really loud."

"Use I."

"I think your actions speak really loud."

"I knew you were full of shit," said Theresa.

"I ran to be with Charlie," Myra said. "That's all. I didn't run because of the program. I didn't use." Wasn't this obvious? Couldn't everyone tell that she scanned the unit for Charlie up and down the hallway, in every room she entered? She glanced at him during meals, Community, Smoke Break. Why couldn't she control herself? Hadn't she gotten what she wanted? Since she had returned, the hands on the clocks moved even slower through her days: Twenty-one. Twenty-two. Twenty-three. Pajamas were excruciating. Jen still hadn't talked to her, but Tina and Lisa had said they were glad Myra was back. Rodney with the zits and large chin, drug of choice paint, hugged her and said he was worried about her. And Victor had sat with her and updated her: he was done with Satan and the whole Satanist movement. He had given up his pentagram necklace, told his parents to give away his T-shirts and take his poster off his bedroom wall.

"It's just a political statement, anyway," he said on Smoke Break. "You were so freaked out about it at first."

"Not really."

Charlie was sitting by Alan with the high voice, drug of choice pot. He was only thirteen. Neither of them were talking.

"I'm glad you're back." Victor's glasses looked like the safety goggles Myra had had to wear in eighth grade shop class.

"Thanks, Victor."

"I told them you wouldn't use. I know you and Charlie are in it for real."

Myra and Charlie. Did he think they were a couple? She prayed for this all the time but then prayed that she would stop praying for this because you didn't pray for yourself. You didn't pray for things you wanted, and whenever Myra did, she felt misguided, that she was ignorant of a fundamental life-understanding. Because God, if He existed—was she suspecting He did? What would her father say?—was like a strict father, always teaching lessons. He did not give you things just because you wanted them. He did not deal in luxurious desires. God withheld.

"You let us down," said Jen. Her voice cracked. A tear dripped onto her slender gold chain, her collarbone. "And Charlie is a leader in the Community. How could you do this to him?"

It was his idea, Myra didn't say.

"Charlie had a role in it, too," said Rachel.

Thank you, Myra didn't say.

"He'll never be focused on his treatment now," said Theresa.

"Myra won't either," said Lisa. "When you have a relationship, it gets in the way of your recovery."

"He's getting so reamed in group," said Abbey, shaking her head, grinning. "Mitch told me."

"You should not be talking about what happens during group to anyone outside of this room. You know this." She turned to Abbey. "You will both face consequences." Rachel sighed. Was she showing frustration? "And we will have a special Community meeting to remind everyone what's lost here when patients choose to gossip. Let's have a think."

Myra had betrayed the Community, jeopardized her recovery and Charlie's. Because she loved him? Or did she love him only because he wanted her? She'd had no feelings for him, none at all, until he'd given her that note. Had she ever had feelings for any boy without his expressing interest? Was that all it took for her to love someone? How did she know if her feelings were real or not? She was so weak. A weak fake piece of shit. She started crying again, praying about it. Praying for relief, happiness, strength—a place to inhabit that was higher than where she was now. Elevated, intangible, impossible.

Silence until Myra reached for her hair and Abbey told her it wasn't okay. Tina crossed her legs. Theresa crossed her arms. Two square buttons on Rachel's phone were flashing.

"So what's lost?" Rachel asked. "Let's go around."

"Trust," said Tina.

"Focus," said Theresa.

"Honesty," said Lisa.

"Nothing," said Abbey.

"Myra?"

"I don't know."

"Sure you do."

"Hope."

"In what?"

"Other people."

"Your turn, Abbey."

She was trying not to scowl. Myra could tell.

"Faith."

"Great. When you have Community tonight, you can each share a sentence or two about what you just said. You're all correct. Tina, are you ready for your final share?" Tina was graduating the next day, returning to her tiny hometown of Tiffin, a dusty, dilapidated, miniature sprawl of buildings along Highway 6 that Myra knew nothing about. Tina was scared shitless. She had told Myra in the bathroom the night before. How was she supposed to keep from hanging out with her using friends? The ones who had written to her, who couldn't wait for her to return and drink with them again? All the patients, after they graduated from Our Primary Purpose, were expected to change their friends. If you want to stay sober, said Rachel, you have to change everything. Where you go and who you go there with. Tina had come up with strategies, plans to meet new people, excuses to make to her current friends—but wouldn't she have to lie to them? Blow them off? Make them hate her?

"Don't I have any consequences?" Myra asked.

"No Contact with Charlie. This includes eye contact. Absolutely none."

"I know that," she said.

"What kind of other consequences were you looking for?" Rachel asked.

They weren't even going to punish her. Not really.

She shrugged.

"You're pathetic," said Theresa.

"That is not okay," said Jen. "Don't talk to people like that."

"Jen's right," said Rachel. "Theresa, why don't you tell Myra how her actions made you feel?"

"I already did."

"Telling someone they're full of shit and pathetic is not a feeling," said Rachel. "Try again."

"You're so quiet. You're like a hurt mouse."

"Use I, please. And you have still not owned one feeling about her actions."

"I feel angry at you."

"Go on."

Theresa shifted in her chair and pulled down her inside-out Motorhead T-shirt. Why wasn't she on a Tuck-In contract? She hid her body all the time.

"I feel like you are not honest with us. About anything. That's why you're so quiet."

"Use I."

"I think that's why you're so quiet. You're a faker."

"Is she right, Myra?"

But I want this, Myra didn't say. I want this thing, this peace. I see it in Lisa, I see it in Jen sometimes, I see it in Rachel. I see it in Erin.

"Kind of."

Rachel nodded. "Tell us how you feel right now."

I want to be with Charlie, she didn't say.

"Guilty," she said. Because that was true, too. Since her return, whenever Jen ignored Myra, Myra felt sorry, responsible. "Scared."

"You hurt me a lot," Jen said. "I was afraid you might die."

"Die?" asked Myra.

"Addicts die when they use," Jen said. "I almost did."

"So did I," said Lisa.

"Do you think you could die if you use, Myra?" asked Rachel.

"I don't know."

"Denial," said Tina.

"Big time," said Jen.

Fuck you, Myra didn't say.

"I want to be sober," Myra said. Because that was true, too.

"Now look at each of us and have a think."

Abbey didn't meet her eye. Her neck was thick and full, but she looked younger than seventeen.

"Abbey, participate, please."

"No," she said.

"I'll take away Smoke Breaks," Rachel said.

Abbey sneered at Myra. Myra knew the sneer was not at her but at Rachel, at pressure and expectation, at how much she probably wanted to drink, smoke pot, snort cocaine—her drug of choice.

Jen cried again. So did Myra. She hated pajamas. They made her feel sedentary. Sick. Like a bath wouldn't help.

"I think how you feel right now is an adequate consequence," said Rachel. Did she know how obsessed she was with Charlie? Counselors knew everything. "Tina, we will do your share after lunch."

"Sorry, Tina," said Myra.

Tina smiled. Myra no longer noticed her teeth every time. "I'm glad you shared. I love you."

"I love you," said Jen.

"I love you," said Myra. Because that was true, too.

Faith

"I don't know where you get this hair," her mother had said when Abbey was small and had allowed herself to be groomed in the mornings before school, sitting atop the washing machine, tights crisp and dress plaid to match, while her mother pulled her hair into a bun, tried to brush down the strays, pin them to her scalp, spray them flat. That was when she'd been a child, good and afraid.

"Oh, Lord!" her mother yelled when she became an adolescent, bad and fearless. Her mother and her father had walked into Abbey's room and discovered Keith on top of her for the third time—he had climbed the lattice like Romeo, snuck into her room.

"My dad took the lock off my door," she'd whispered as his hand went up her shirt.

"I can be quick," he said, kissing her kid-nipple, pushing her in place on the Raggedy Ann and Andy bedspread. "I love you."

"I love you, too," she said, opening herself to him, closing her eyes, Night Ranger in her head.

Then, boom. Keith off her and out the window, her mother pointing at Abbey's unzipped jeans like they were the star of Satan, and her father running after him, a pudgy bald dad-blob in the streetlights, screaming for someone to call the police. Keith always parked his truck four blocks away and her father couldn't run more than a foot.

"Were you having sex, young lady?" He said, when he returned. He was panting. He sat her down at the kitchen table and shook his finger at her. Abbey's father wanted their family to be good. A center of morality.

Right! Said the real estate agent who sold rich people gigantic homes on golf courses and bought her family a second Cadillac. They drove to church as if part of a parade, shiny shoes on display, fake-jeweled clip holding up Abbey's difficult hair, coarse and wiry and unwilling to bend.

"So what if I was?"

"Are you drunk?" said her mother.

"Maybe," said Abbey. High, not drunk. Idiot.

"I'm calling Father Xavier," he said. "This cannot go on. I cannot control her."

Her mother crossed herself like Italians in mafia movies, like the nuns at Abbey's Catholic school. As if that did anything. Abbey was heading to hell and she knew it, and when she wasn't high the fear of it pushed her into prayer. At her desk in class, on her knees in bathroom stalls, alone in her room after Keith left, her body warm and crumpled.

But when she was high she forgot about all the places her sins could take her. Or maybe she just didn't care as much, snorting it up, swallowing it down, inhaling it hard as conviction and pride were lifted, gently and quietly and quickly removed.

Systems

Myra should pray, but she didn't want to. She wanted to feel that rush of warmth when Charlie entered a room and smiled at her before he sat down, the way that smile made her certain he was thinking about her, desiring her, his hair soft brown and his eyebrows just a little too dark. Smoke Break was still fifteen minutes away. Myra sat at the window in the lounge with two cigarettes in the pocket of her robe. She closed her eyes. Hi, God. But then she opened her eyes because she felt embarrassed that other patients would think she was praying and deceitful that her heart was not in it. Sometimes she felt like she was praying to nothing. Was manufacturing belief part of belief? Hadn't Bliss said that—fake it till you make it? Maybe this is what serenity was: pretending. Acting like you believed and hoping that you would. Eventually.

But what if you never really felt it?

From across the room, Victor announced that Chris was leaving.

"He's running?" Myra asked. He was Chris with the crew cut, drug of choice Jim Beam. He had arrived on Myra's Day Fifteen.

Victor shook his head. He sat beside Ron, who was better, less weavy and shaky but closing his eyes like a monk at all times of day to pray. Rodney said Russell Dean had had to order him not to pray in Small Group.

God isn't going anywhere, he had said. *You can reach Him later.*

"Chris is packing right now," said Victor. "They're discharging him." Tina, who sat in the wide sill of the picture window, scoffed. Abbey and Sam nodded.

"I don't get it," Myra said.

"He's not chemically dependent," Jen said.

"You don't actually believe that," Victor said.

"They diagnosed him," Jen said.

"I bet his insurance wouldn't cover treatment," Victor said.

"That didn't matter," Jen said.

"It's all a scam," said Victor. "Why do you think the limit is sixty days? Insurance. It costs a shit-ton of money to be in here. And they let us in because our parents have money."

Myra's house needed painting and the car they drove was falling apart. She didn't have any fur coats or Guess jeans. They didn't have a nice house by City High with a pool and their sofa was Naugahyde. And Lisa was in foster care and Tina had the crookedest teeth Myra had ever seen. Nobody there was rich.

"But I talked to Bliss about it," Jen said. "They were not convinced he was chemically dependent. It can be situational sometimes."

"You're so stupid," Victor said.

"That's not okay," Myra said to him.

"Bliss lies. They all do. What do you think addict kids without insurance do?"

"No one lies," said Myra.

"They lie every day," said Victor. "This is all political."

Myra pictured secret phone calls. Hotlines directly to Ronald Reagan.

"Stop it!" said Jen.

Abbey and Sam left the lounge to ask to get cigarettes from their rooms. Not everyone carried them around and played with them all day or pretended to smoke them between groups.

"I heard his Tell-All," said Victor. "He is chemically dependent as hell."

Jen stood up, feet tiny in her Reeboks. "If they say he's not chemically dependent, then he isn't! You're not a doctor!"

"Neither are they," he said.

"They consult doctors," Jen said. "They work with doctors."

"So they say."

"Shut up! You're ruining everything!"

"I need a cigarette," he said. Patients said that all day long like workers aging and tired.

"There he is," said Victor, nodding to where he stood with Bliss and Russell Dean at the door to the unit. Chris carried his suitcase.

They all stared.

"They're really going to let him go," Victor said.

Bliss and Russell Dean were speaking to him intently. Bliss had her slender, elbowy arms crossed. She looked grave, but she always looked grave, as if worry had settled forever into her forehead.

Jen marched over.

"I can't believe you're leaving," she said. "We were just getting to know you."

"Yeah," Chris said, glancing at Russell Dean. "I guess I don't have anything to worry about."

"You'll be okay," said Russell Dean.

"You shouldn't go," said Victor.

"You are not qualified to make that decision," said Russell Dean.

"This is bullshit."

"Think about arrogance, Victor. Where has it gotten you?" Victor's eyes reddened. He blinked.

"High in the gutter with your mom and dad frantic. That's where." Russell Dean was talking about the last time Victor had run away, his second time. Yeah, he had used, he told the Community. The urges were too much. Nothing helped. Not talking about them or playing the tape all the way through or writing about it or praying. The urges were so bad he didn't care what would happen.

"I mean," he had asked the circle. "What if you want to use no matter what you do?"

Russell Dean put his hand on Chris's shoulder. "You can trust us, Victor."

"Clean up your side of the street, Victor," said Bliss. "Your side."

Jen hugged Chris. Other patients emerged from the smoke room, where they had been packing their individual cigarettes on the tables, the sounds like drumming fingers. They took turns saying goodbye.

"So you're not an alcoholic?" asked Myra. His face was so white, popped here and there with moles.

"I guess not," he said. "I can't wait to go home."

And you're going to drink? Like you were never here? Myra didn't ask.

"Take care of yourself, buddy," said Victor.

"I put my address in there," said Charlie, pointing to the *Big Book* Chris held in one hand. Myra made sure not to look at Charlie's face. She hoped he was doing the same. He was one of the senior patients now—fewer than ten days left.

"So did I," said Bryan.

"Me, too," said Rodney.

"You know where we are," said Bliss.

Russell Dean led Chris out of the unit. The single bell rang—the start of Smoke Break.

"Is he going to be okay?" asked Myra.

"They're not going to let anyone go if it isn't safe," said Jen.

In the smoke room, Jen led the first verse of "Beth," the only Kiss song by drummer Peter Criss, but Myra did not want to sing. Her stomach hurt a little and her throat was dry and she did not want her cigarette but lit it anyway and exhaled with that sigh of relief that all of them let out when they finally got to have nicotine after hours of deprivation. In one corner, Charlie sat with Victor and Rodney. No one looked at Myra. Outside, the late day sunlight was barely yellow, that faded color through the window that confirmed for them the time of day was changing.

Conversion

It was time for Abbey's Own Up. She had refused to pick anyone from Small Group to be her peer support, so Rachel told Myra she could get out of pajamas a day early to go with Abbey to the meeting.

"It'll be okay," Myra said as they walked side by side down the hallway. Smooth walls, hospital gray. Carpet that appeared dark blue, but when you studied it for only a few seconds you could see the speckles—light blue, brown, pale red.

Abbey was trembling, her left eyelid twitching like it did in group.

"It's really hard, but it'll be okay," Myra said. She put her arm around Abbey's shoulders. "I love you." And she meant it.

"Sure you do, Treatment Head."

Myra took her arm away and started to sweat. Use I. "I feel hurt by what you just said."

"Good for you." Abbey opened the conference room door. There sat Rachel, as if she were meditating with her eyes open; Russell Dean, who wore a navy tie; Abbey's mother, in a ruffled blouse with her hair swept up and her bangs curled under; Abbey's father, who wore jeans and an Izod shirt; and Abbey's two siblings, both blond boys, one sitting in his mother's lap sucking his thumb, and the other holding a baseball cap. He jumped down from his chair and ran to Abbey. No one else did.

"Hey, Champie," she said, hugging him. He ran back to his mother.

Rachel opened the meeting by telling Abbey's family that she was glad Abbey was here at Our Primary Purpose. They were glad to see the whole family because Abbey needed them—she had used more drugs than any of them had been aware of.

"Oh no," her mother said. "Oh dear." She started to cry.

Rachel clasped her hands on the conference table.

"Do you want to take it from here, Abbey, or should I?"

Myra saw Abbey swallow, her Adam's apple like a Super Ball.

"Tell them your drug of choice."

"Cocaine." The last syllable was high, the cadence of a question, as Abbey put her hands over her face. The word filled the room. Her father put his hands on his knees. Abbey's younger little brother wailed and slid off his mother's lap and ran to Abbey, who was weeping, trying to catch air. Abbey scooped him up and rocked him.

"I'm sorry, buddy," Abbey said. "I'm sorry. I'll never do it again. I promise. I'm sorry."

"Thank God you're here," her father said, blowing his nose. "Thank God. We are blessed."

Myra stared at Abbey as she cried. Her parents had had no idea? These homely, attentive-seeming people? Were they gone every night? Myra understood that she was watching another version of Abbey's story, another version of Abbey that no one else in OPP had seen: unpolished, scared, remorseful. Rachel had laid it bare.

***

In Community that night after dinner, Abbey finally shared. "I hurt my kid brothers. I babysat them wasted so many times."

"You're sick," said Bryan. "You have a disease."

"I'm totally glad you're talking, Abbey," said Jen. "I was so scared for you."

"Pray," said Mitch. Myra rolled her eyes. Faker.

"I hurt my little sister," said Bryan. He was on Day Thirty-two. "I... I got my sister stoned when she was seven." Patients gazed at the top of his head as he spoke, a sloppy part in the middle. "I don't know how I could do that. So sick." He blinked—a tear splatted on the carpet. "She fell down the stairs and broke her arm. I drove her to the hospital drunk. Puked all over my dad's truck when I got to the E.R."

Wow, Myra didn't say. I don't know how anyone could do that, either. But no one ever said such things. No one passed judgment if you confessed something—only if you didn't.

"She forgives me," Bryan said. "They all say they do. Because I'm going to change." Bryan sat up fully straight—he was tall and lean. He wore an inside-out Jethro Tull T-shirt and jeans. "I mean, I am changing. So are you, Abbey. You can do it."

"Glad you're here, Abbey," said Charlie. He was on Day Forty-six. He wore a plaid shirt with a collar tucked into Levi's, battered Top Siders. He was the leader of Community tonight. Techs only looked in sometimes, usually during a patient's How You Got Here. Otherwise, the patients with the most days in treatment did the directing.

"Glad you're here," said Lisa.

"Glad you're here, Abbey," said Myra. She stared at Charlie. Nothing. Then for the first time since they returned, Charlie looked at her and smiled. Hugely. Lovingly. As if he didn't care who saw.

His smile felt like an act that resulted from something. Had she worried so much about Charlie's feelings for her that God was finally showing her how Charlie loved her? He brushed his long hair over one shoulder and straightened his back. He still hadn't looked away. Myra felt God fill her up, as if she had been empty her whole life.

***

Myra started carrying her *Big Book* with her. She read it in the study carrel every morning after she finished homework, in the lounge with her feet up on the wide windowsill after Smoke Breaks, at the desk in her room before lights out. She underlined sentences, paragraphs, and passages because if the words on the page triggered any emotion, they might have the potential to change her. The words became answers to questions she already had and those she could not articulate. Paths toward serenity.

In the first part of the *Big Book* were the whys. Why you were an alcoholic, why you had no control, why you had become a destructive wreck. The chapters that followed explained how to work the program, how to complete the Twelve Steps, how to change your life. In the white space that started and ended some of these chapters, Myra had taken notes during Margaret's lectures. Above the start of "The Doctor's Opinion," a letter written in 1938 by William D. Silkworth on his professional view of alcoholism as a disease beyond the alcoholic's control, Myra wrote: "Disease (alcoholism)—a condition that separates a person from normal patterns of health; chronic (long term); incurable; treatable; progressive; fatal. This is ME. I RISKED MY LIFE TO GET DRUNK." And wasn't this true? After she'd tried to kill herself—or done whatever she had that night—her psychiatrist and her neuropsychologist had told Myra not to drink on Elavil. That it could stop her heart.

She remembered waking up one Saturday on a wicker loveseat. Myra's left leg was asleep. Her cheek was pressed against the rattan weave of the armrest, her neck bent and her head throbbing. On the wall above Myra, coming into focus, was a framed picture of a boy and a girl in overalls fishing in a rowboat, the countryside around them shaded in different hues of brown. She became aware of her heart, which had never beat with such force—it pulsed in her ears and every squish of her brain. She opened her mouth, lifted her head from the armrest. She needed to vomit. Her saliva was like paste.

How had she gotten here? She sat up and looked quickly around the room. The house was silent. A school picture of Bonnie—super-popular Bonnie, in the top tier, one of the giants—smiled from a bookcase shelf and Myra realized she must be at Bonnie's house. Why hadn't she gone home? Did her father know where she was?

The night before had begun at a City High football game: Little Hawks vs. Solon. It would be a blowout, Mark had assured Myra. They were together then, but he had not asked her to leave the game early, find his Trans Am in the City High parking lot, and wait in the passenger seat while he showered. This was what they had always done. She didn't know why they weren't doing their routine, and to keep from seeming insecure she didn't ask why not and made plans to go to the game with Cindy and Bonnie.

It was mid-November, cold. In the floodlights that arched over the football field Myra saw mists of drizzle slanting down. In the bleachers couples and families sat on cushions with waterproof covers, wearing thick warm clothes under rain slickers, holding one up to cover themselves and the cooler between them. Why had they come? Not all of them had children on the team or cheerleading squad or in the marching band. Why did they care so much? (If

God does exist, her father always said, He doesn't give a shit about football.)

Myra was freezing in her turtleneck and sweater. A jacket would have looked stupid, and she didn't own a raincoat—just a thick winter coat, which also looked stupid. Myra hated winter. She did not know how to stay warm, how to dress for cold, how to stay dry. A hat or a hood would have disturbed her hair clips and barrettes, and girls avoided hats anyway to protect the style of their hair, sprayed into long wings. The bleacher was full of feathered heads, each one coated in tiny, delicate droplets. Girl-birds. Her hands were getting numb; Cindy and Bonnie wore mittens and jackets and talked while Myra shivered and thought about Mark. What would he do after the game? Would he call her tomorrow? What should she do if he didn't? Call him? She wanted beer, which she knew they would drink later, but later was never ever soon enough.

The game ended and Bonnie drove them to Lance's house. He was a twenty-three-year-old City High graduate, standing on his front stoop in only gym shorts despite the cold, his torso thick and muscled in the light over his front door. Weeds grew from the ground to the bottom of his single-wide trailer. Van Halen erupted from giant speakers. So much beer. Bud Light and Coors and forty-ouncers of Michelob. Cindy and Bonnie danced in the center of Lance's living room while Myra sat on the couch. Cindy waved. Myra waved back and smoked cigarettes and flicked into a dirty plastic cup and drank. A lot.

"You smoke?" said Bonnie, taking a break, sitting beside her.

"Sometimes," said Myra. She blinked in slow motion. She liked smoking—it made her feel powerful and glamourous, tapping the ash or flicking it if you wanted to appear unmoved, like you didn't care. Stomping the butt into the ground. Lots of girls smoked: popular or unpopular, greasy or groomed. Pulling out a pack of Marlboro Light 100s and flipping open the box-top made a statement. As if you were either in absolute charge of your life, keeping a secret, or running from something. All three narratives were a lure.

"Doesn't Mark hate smoking?"

"I hardly ever do it."

"I think it's gross." She got up and pushed Cindy and Lance into each other, laughing, tried to convince Cindy to make out with him, to follow him down that narrow, paneled hallway into his bedroom.

And then Myra woke up on the loveseat. She walked down the hallway and opened the door to what she guessed was Bonnie's room—there she was, Cindy sleeping in the double bed beside her. They had put her on the couch? Who had driven them home? Had Mark tried to find her? She looked down at herself, searched the pockets of her jeans. She went to the bathroom across the hall and looked in the mirror. Her cheek was imprinted with crisscross rattan weaves. She felt for the bobby pins at the back of her neck—still there. She felt a separation from her last-night self. A before and after. A departure from one self into another.

Had she been stupid? Had all her fears emerged? Did everyone now know who she really was?

She walked to Bonnie's kitchen and drank a glass of water and rinsed out her mouth. Through the window over the kitchen sink was a green lawn, a robin perched on the edge of an empty stone birdbath. Was that a robin? No—they migrated in winter. Why didn't Myra *know* anything?

Her father. Did he know where she was? She picked up Bonnie's phone and dialed the number.

"Hi, Dad." She was trembling.

"Hello, Love. You coming home early?"

She swallowed. "Not yet."

"Last night you said noon."

"Right."

"The Nova giving you any trouble?" Had she driven it? No, no. They'd been in Bonnie's car. Everything was okay. Everything was okay. Everything was okay.

"No. I mean, I haven't tried to start it yet."

"Mark called."

Had she talked to him? But he had called her, so everything was okay. Everything was okay. Everything was okay.

"I'll let you know if it doesn't start."

Had that been God? Keeping her safe? Everybody there said that God had been looking out for them; that's why they weren't dead. Or in jail. Or in a mental hospital.

What about the people who did die? Myra heard the question, like a pause between thoughts. She quickly opened her *Big Book* and on the inside cover, she wrote

IF I DRINK I WILL DIE

ASK GOD FOR HELP, MYRA

✓✓STOP HOLDING THINGS IN✓✓

This is YOU, Myra, don't forget it.

I am not weak, I am ill

In the second part of the *Big Book*, alcoholics wrote their stories. Whether she could apply their experiences or not, whether the stories began in 1904 or 1934, whether the narrator was an author, deacon, doctor, executive, waitress, Christian, or housewife—each of the stories was very important and absolutely true in Myra's life, too. Myra found a way to relate to every single narrator: man (almost all of them were), woman, young adult, geriatric. Myra forced connections with them all. Lots of them—the ones who could afford to—had been so unable stop drinking that they admitted themselves to asylums, a word Myra associated with the 1800s, with Dr. Jekyll and Mr. Hyde or Edgar Allen Poe. She pictured grey concrete buildings full of rooms with examination tables, beds covered in white sheets and patients in dirty gowns, wandering, disheveled, and moaning. Drafty hallways, a sprawling cellar with a dungeon of death like Fortunato's room in "A Cask of Amontillado."

Myra wrote, THIS COULD BE ME.

***

Myra was trying to sleep and couldn't; she thought without mercy of Charlie. Did he like her? Love her? Think of her? Long for her? If she talked herself into yes, she rose up to elation; if she talked herself into no, she fell into despair. Over and over and over. She blinked at the light from the hallway that slitted through her door, got on her knees, pressed her palms together, and begged for relief. To turn it over. She said amen and then grabbed her hair.

Is this what God would want me to do?

She let it go. Then she thought of Erin.

In bare feet, Myra went to her, dark hallway leading to the light of the nurses' station. On this floor of the unit the workspace was bare, the wall shelves and cabinets and file drawers mostly empty.

"I want to pull out my hair." Because this was true, too.

"You do that, don't you?" Erin asked. She had a tiny jaw. Light from her reading lamp hit the desk shelf in a blurry trapezium, a shape in the dark. "I read it in your chart."

Myra nodded.

"Have you prayed?"

"Over and over."

"You need to let God in there. Let's pray together."

They held hands and kneeled at the desk. Erin opened her *Big Book* to the Third Step prayer and placed it before Myra so they could recite together:

God, I offer myself to Thee—to build with me and do with me as Thou wilt. Relieve me of the bondage of self, that I may better do Thy will. Take away my difficulties, that victory over them may bear witness to those I would help of Thy Power, Thy Love, and Thy Way of life. May I do Thy will always!

Myra's voice was just above a whisper. She worried that one of the girls would come out. Wouldn't someone hear them? Her face burned in the dark, her hands clammy as she pressed her palms together.

When they finished, Erin hugged Myra.

"You're special, you know that?" Myra hugged her back, absorbed the sincerity, thanked her. It didn't matter what Charlie thought, what anyone thought. She needed to focus on herself. She needed to be better.

"Read that *Big Book*," said Erin. "You'll find yourself."

Who she wanted to be was approaching. A boat parting the waters. A cowboy on horseback riding through a mountain pass. A pioneer cutting through tall grass.

***

Rachel assigned her Step Two: She was to define her Higher Power. It could be whatever she wanted it to be; it didn't have to be God. So Myra read Chapter 4, "We Agnostics," which told her that she had always believed and needed to capture this certainty.

"JUST STOP DOUBTING," she wrote. "FEELINGS DON'T COME FROM LOGIC." If only she could think about the certainty of God and nothing else for long enough, change it from concept to trust, breathe it in like oxygen, touch it like a dandelion. But all she envisioned was a tall white man with a long white beard and a long white gown. In the clouds, on a throne. Like a wizard.

Myra had officially prayed to Him for the first time when she was seven. After dinner, instead of watching TV while Keen graded papers, she pulled a small red candle from the back corner of a neglected kitchen drawer. She lit it, dripped the wax into a saucer, twisted the candle into place. She paused and looked down the basement stairs to make sure Keen wasn't coming in to load the dishwasher, wasn't noticing that she was creating an altar instead of watching *Charlie's Angels*. Keen was an atheist in a foxhole, so she'd have to sneak it—praying in her mind wouldn't be enough. It had to matter. God had to hear. She carried the candle to her room, her hand shielding the flame like actors did in historical TV movies; she felt so grown-up and matronly and elegant, as if she were about to order a servant to get the milking done, prepare the roast, polish the silver. It was winter. The dry, furnaced heat flowed out through the vents; the wind blew the shades from the windows like sheets on a clothesline. The snow outside was piling into drifts; there might not be school tomorrow.

She turned off the lamp on her bedside table and made her altar so God would know that she was serious. She was, wasn't she? Maybe not, since she never prayed before. God must have known that in her soul, Myra was not serious, not devoted enough. So she had to make it official. She placed on her desk the candle, a cross she had cut from an empty cereal box and colored yellow for gold, and the picture of her mother smiling on the porch, her arms spread between the posts.

God, please make my mother come back, even though I know she can't. Myra kneeled and held herself like a nun she'd seen on *Vegas*. Was her mother beside her, reaching for a hug? Myra could smell her scented lotion, feel the delicacy of her skin she said came from too much sunbathing as a teenager, see her pale face, her unruly hair. She spoke. The image was so vivid that Myra reached for it like a child in a Sunday-funnies daydream, petting the air as if she were reaching for a horse or a goat in a petting zoo. She slumped into a z on her knees, gazed at the candle, then straightened and pledged to pray every day from now on.

The wizard in the sky received prayers through a ticker-tape machine, glass dome shining bright as a star beside him on a wooden table, unless it was shielded by clouds of clean and perfect whiteness. The machine was never silent, clicking like a million clocks, like the opening of *CBS Nightly News*. God ignored, rejected, or fulfilled each prayer, his God-hands holding the ticker tape, his God-eyes reading some and not others, depending on the gravity of the prayer, the earnestness of the human. Did she mean it? Did she believe? Was she good? And sometimes His assessments didn't matter, because if He granted too many in a row He had to reject or ignore the next set to maintain or project the appearance of fairness. Rarely, almost never, did He pause in this process since there were so many prayers at once. There was not time.

But wouldn't He pause for Myra? Lean forward and look over the ticker tape and down at the earth, find her because she was special? Or maybe He gave individual consideration to each person only one time. Because everyone was special. The wind whined around the corners of their house; her window shade flickered in a draft. That must be a sign. God was there, demonstrating His power. Myra just knew she was heard. She had to be.

But why had nothing changed? Why did she still suffer so much if He had really heard her? Why did everyone suffer so much?

She needed Him more than ever now. She had to rely on a Higher Power (which everyone called God) to change her patheticness into confidence, to keep from feeling afraid, to stay sober. She knew the wizard she had tried to believe in was silly and childish; Myra was able, sometimes, to dismiss this vision. A giant man in the sky was physically impossible. But she was unable to question the process, the choosing-from-above who received grace and who did not. The imposed randomness felt accurate; she didn't want to believe in it, but she did, and she could not admit or articulate this. Instead, she decided to start over, begin belief anew. So Myra asked all the counselors and techs what her Higher Power could be.

"A chair," said Rachel.

"A doorknob," said Bliss.

"It can be a tree. It can be a fucking vaporizer," said Russell Dean.

"A river," said Grace.

"A lamppost. A star," said Margaret.

"A feeling," said Erin. "Like love." And this was the one Myra chose. When she prayed, which was now morning and night on her knees and throughout the day in her mind, she prayed for love to help her: to take away her obsessions, her worry, her fear.

But what she still saw was the wizard, spreading his arms, hood sleeves expanding in a white mass as he spread arms across the immortal sky and blocked out the clouds.

"Fake it till you make it," said Jen. And Myra did. She would do anything. It's not as if all the counselors were lying. They wouldn't lie to her about the program, about how to work it, about how it had worked for them. They were good, happy people. Bliss might be distant, Russell Dean might be cold, but of course they had serenity. Of course they did. They wouldn't have their jobs if they didn't have serenity and work a program. And Rachel, too— but only for her food addiction. Weren't all the counselors and techs… correct, more or less? Didn't the program make sense in a lot of ways? Wouldn't her confidence grow, her depression lift, her self-esteem rise, and her desperation ease? It's not as if they were lying. They cared about her. They wanted her to get better, to stop pulling out her hair, to stop being so susceptible.

She began to hug. She hugged the patients she wanted to hug and the patients she didn't want to hug. Girls, boys, it didn't matter. In treatment, patients hugged one another after groups, before bed, during one-on-ones. When a new patient arrived, Myra plopped herself into an empty chair beside them and smiled. "I'm glad you're here," she'd say, putting her hand on the new patient's shoulder. She said *I love you* more and more. To Erin, Jen, Abbey, Tina after her last Community, and to Lisa and Theresa, who were now the senior patients. And the more she said it, the more she felt loved. Jen was right. The program was working.

***

The night before Charlie graduated, Abbey snuck Myra's *Big Book* to him so he could sign it. Patients signed *Big Books* like yearbooks, handwriting of all sizes and contours scribbled on the inside covers and the white space at chapter beginnings and ends. He drew a sketch of her face in pencil, colored in shadow and made her eyes larger than they were, her hair longer and straighter, with no images of hair clips.

Myra:

Meeting you has been one of the best things to happen to me. I learned so much from You. I will never, as long as I live, forget what we had. You are a very special person & You mean so much to me. What we had was great. I realy hope You keep up the good work & do the best You can in treatment. I want to wish You the best of Luck & happiness in The Rest of Your Life. You desirve it. I love you—Charlie DeLong.

He does love me. Myra sat up in bed before lights out, covers up to her waist, the overhead light on since the patient rooms had no lamps. She put the *Big Book* beside her pillow, turned out the light, and prayed to have all thoughts of him removed, to focus on herself instead. She was wrong to focus on him. Wrong, wrong, wrong. She was weak, afraid, insecure, unable to get to God's will. Damn her!

Maybe he didn't love her. Was there any way to know for sure?

Cycles

Lori, a new patient with short hair and an ankle bracelet, drug of choice pot, was giving her Tell-All.

"What about cocaine?" asked Theresa.

"Never."

"Liar," said Theresa.

"Lori," said Rachel. "Think carefully about what you're telling your group right now."

"I am," said Lori.

"She's good," said Abbey.

Myra kept her arms crossed and stared at the floor, knowing she could offer nothing because of what had happened when she went home for her one-time weekend pass, which all patients got around Day Forty. Myra blinked and sat harder on her hands.

Keen had picked Myra up in a rental car. The Nova had been sitting in the driveway since Myra left.

"Haven't tried to start it," said Keen, flicking his cigarette butt out the cracked window. Myra watched it shoot across the door glass and disappear. "We're going to have to get a new car."

"You should put them out in the ashtray, Dad," she said. "That's how holes get into the backseat." She had never told Keen what to do before.

"Oh, I'm careful," he said, punching the car lighter into the receptacle above the ashtray.

I've been sober thirty-eight days, she didn't say. Because approval didn't matter if you had to ask for it. So many unstated rules that nobody made.

The lighter popped out. He removed it and held the heating element against his cigarette and puffed.

"Can I have one?" she asked.

Keen raised his eyebrows.

"Remember what your grandmother said about smoking?"

"Never start."

"That's right."

"She said that while she lit up."

He chuckled. "I suppose you're right." He held out the package. Generics.

As she took the cigarette out of the pack, she took her first drag in front of her father and saw herself doing it. This way of watching her life, inspecting everything she did, left her always afraid of doing or saying something that was wrong, that would embarrass her, that would unearth her obsessive watching. She flicked into the ashtray and felt elegant and mature and wise like an adult but also guilty, aware that she should not be smoking. Why hadn't Keen's permission made a difference? Why couldn't she welcome this invitation into his life?

He had taken her straight to Felix and Oscar's for her favorite pizza in Iowa City, baked in a cast iron pan with cheese right on the crust and thick sauce on top. They took a window table on State Street and watched university students walk by in the dusk.

"I've been sober thirty-eight days," she finally said.

"I'm so glad," he said. "It will be nice to have you back in the house."

She sipped her Coke.

"I believe in God now."

He pulled out the *Press-Citizen*, the Iowa City newspaper, and placed it on the table in front of him.

"Now why would you do *that*?"

"The program won't work unless you believe in God," she said.

"I wasn't aware that OPP was religious."

"It's not. They don't use the Bible or anything."

"I see."

"You have to have a Higher Power if you want to be sober. I choose God for mine. That's just easier."

He pulled his glasses from his shirt pocket and exhaled on them, rubbed them with the napkin.

"Are you going to be all right now?"

I don't know, Myra didn't say. I'm too afraid not to try.

"Yes," she said. "Definitely. This is what I've needed all my life."

"Well, good," he said.

She felt like a child. She didn't know what else to say. There was space between them that he should have filled but never did. It was always up to her to make conversation with her father, and it wasn't fair. This invisible burden. It made her feel like she had to figure out how and when and why to say the simplest of things. Like she was being interrogated when she wasn't.

It was Jen's turn. She wanted *another* consultation on her Fourth Step—the searching and fearless moral inventory. She held her legal pad up like a sideways rectangle and showed everyone the columns she had drawn.

"Don't I need more columns?" Jen asked. "Like 'How I Was Selfish?' or 'How My Low Self-Esteem Affected My Mom?'"

"Wouldn't you do that in the 'What Was My Part' column?" asked Lisa. She was on Day Fifty-four, giving her Fifth Step to Rachel in a few days.

"That's what I'm doing," said Theresa.

"I'm making a list," said Lisa.

"What if my part wasn't selfish?" Jen asked. "What if I didn't mean to hurt someone?"

"It's still your part," said Rachel. "The fourth step is about self-centeredness, not just selfishness. The two are alike but different."

Jen started writing. The sound of pen on paper whisked through the room. "I get it. I get it. I know how to do it. I got it. I'm so self-absorbed! I wish I could stop thinking about myself! Jeez!"

Of course Myra was thinking about herself, too, because on her pass home she had slipped. Had a relapse. Gotten drunk. Nancy had been excited that she was coming and said so in a letter, drawn hearts down the sides of the white notebook paper and colored them in with red pen.

You can stay over, K? I won't drink or anything. We can watch movies and have Pagliai's sausage and mushroom. Cooper and Dave can just be somewhere else, cuz they'll bring beer and be stupid. Maybe I'll bake a cake for you!!!!! And we can go cruzin' in the Nova!

"Myra," Rachel finally said. "How was your weekend?"

After pizza with Keen, she had gone to an AA meeting. That had been okay. She had rehearsed.

"I'm Myra, and I'm an alcoholic," she said.

"Hi, Myra," they all said back. They looked curious, smiling at her from around the large table; chairs also lined the walls. She felt from them an eagerness to know her. It was almost overwhelming, their desire, from the man with the parted hair and the polyester slacks and the thick belt, the Vietnam veteran who read his own short poetry, the woman with gray hair to her waist who pulled up on a motorcycle, the man in the dirty T-shirt and cutoffs with the pockets showing, the two women sitting against the windowed front wall who dressed like bank tellers and chewed tobacco while everyone else smoked cigarettes, filling the air. Myra felt at ease. She could do nothing wrong, nothing to displease them.

"I'm on a weekend home from treatment," Myra said. Three more sentences plus the thank you. "I'll be here tomorrow night, too. I'm supposed to get some phone numbers for when I get out. God and the program have changed my life. Thank you."

"Thanks, Myra." They smiled, and Myra felt pressure, a twinge of repulsion, then elation. She didn't understand the vacillations, the way she sped from one feeling to its opposite so quickly that it made her discredit herself, doubt her own sincerity, feel such permanence in each one.

God help her.

"I slipped," Myra said, eyes still on the floor.

Jen gasped. "Why didn't you tell me?"

"*You* slipped?" asked Abbey.

"I don't know."

"What happened?"

"I drank. I got drunk," Myra said.

"She's only telling us because her piss test will be positive," said Theresa.

"Say that directly to Myra, please," said Rachel.

"I think you're only telling us because your piss test will be positive."

"No, she's not," said Lisa.

"I am so scared for you," said Jen. "I am so scared. You are totally holding back right now."

"Did you go to a meeting?" asked Jen.

"Friday," Myra said.

"Saturday?"

Myra shook her head. She had planned to. She backed out of the driveway, but when she got to the corner her hands turned the steering wheel the other way. She went to Nancy's early instead. Nancy already had the basement all set up, and Myra asked her for a beer, because she knew Nancy had some.

"What?" Nancy said. "No way."

"Please?" Myra said.

"We are not drinking tonight! Don't you need to go to AA or something?" Nancy's dad was in the program. He lived in Illinois and Nancy talked to him on the phone sometimes. He mailed her presents.

"I went last night," said Myra. She had a list of numbers in her purse. Roxanne, Meg, Lizette. But she wasn't thinking of calling them because she was going to drink. Period. So she erected a barrier that other options could not pass through, colossal as life and real as a wall of steel, cement, pressurized planks of wood. Solid in her chest like actual matter.

"I don't remember what happened," Myra said.

"It's more important to understand what happened *before* you slipped," said Rachel.

She'd walked out Nancy's front door.

"Myra, don't!" Nancy called from her stoop. Concrete, with two stairs to the sidewalk. "You'll be so sorry!"

"I'll be right back," Myra said. She could wait outside the 7-Eleven and ask someone to buy her beer. She had done it once with Cindy, asking herself why an adult would do such a thing and then dismissing the question. Over and over.

Then Dave had pulled up in his dad's Chevette. Myra stopped in the middle of Nancy's front yard, the lawn patched with brown. Dave had an Iowa Hawkeye cap on backward with a bandana tied at the back of his neck. A tight white T-shirt. He played football.

"Fuck!" Nancy yelled. "Go away, Dave! You're not supposed to come over! Asshole!"

"What the hell, Nance?" he called.

"Can you get me some beer, Dave?" asked Myra.

"You bet, girl! Come on! Let's go to my house."

She drank those first beers fast. Cooper was there, too, and she took a shot of tequila from him. She also took a shot of peppermint schnapps from Dave's friend Steve. Girls were there, too, juniors and seniors she didn't know, and she sat on the couch and drank beers very quickly and watched them standing in the corner by a glassed-in cabinet of trophies, tiny metal limbs glinting in the light. Were the girls not looking at her on purpose? Were they pretending she was not there?

"I blacked out," said Myra.

"Everybody has," said Abbey.

"No. Not everybody," said Rachel. "I have never blacked out in my life. None of my friends have ever blacked out. Only sick people drink until they don't remember what they did. You all are sick; do you understand that?"

"Be careful," Dave said, watching her pull open another beer. He smiled. "I don't want to have to carry you out of here." They were in Dave's basement. She was sitting on the floor now. She ran her hand back and forth over the soft fibers of plush maroon carpet and watched the color change. From a sofa, the girls were now watching her. Outside the sliding glass door was a sloped backyard, rich green in the dusk. Pink Floyd played. All the secrets in Iowa happened in basements.

Rachel leaned forward. "Do you know why you didn't go to that meeting, why you drank? Why you're not telling us everything right now, when you know you should?"

Because I'm afraid, she didn't say. Because I cannot handle things.

"I bet you had phone numbers in your pocket."

Something emerged. A surge of insistence from what might have been Myra's ribs. From what might have been.

"Because I miss my mom?" She couldn't locate her voice. Her throat felt closed.

Rachel raised her eyebrows. An expression at last.

"Your mom?" asked Jen. "I thought she died a long time ago."

"Your mom died?" asked Theresa.

"You still think about your mom?" asked Lisa.

"My mom died, too," said Lori. "Last year. I think about her all the time."

Myra put her face over her hands and wept.

Nancy to the rescue. That's what Myra had said to her the next morning, when she woke up in Nancy's basement, back in the waterbed with MTV. Duran Duran on a beach, an island, in pursuit of a human sand-wolf with a painted body.

"Cooper came over and I had him drive me over there. Everyone else was about to leave. Dave would've fucked you. Awake or passed out. He'd fuck anything. Dead, alive, animal, mineral. He's gross. I keep telling Cooper that."

"I don't remember," Myra said.

"You need to go back to treatment," Nancy said.

"Are you mad at me?"

Nancy shook her head. "I know how someone gets when they want to drink."

Myra wouldn't tell them that, who she had become, storming out into the world but staying behind her barrier at the same time.

"That's good," said Rachel. "Very, very good, Myra."

"Okay," Myra said.

"You need to share your relapse with the Community tonight. That is your responsibility. You also need to call your father and tell him."

"You'll drink if you don't," said Jen.

"Why?" asked Abbey.

"Addicts aren't honest," said Rachel. "They don't own up when they lie. They feel guilty for it, then they use. It's a cycle, like a circle." Rachel made one in the air with her index finger and looked at Myra. "Sometimes a trip home helps us see it."

Myra was sweating. All her fear had turned to water, excreting, soaking the earth.

"Addicts can't have secrets." Rachel looked at Myra. "And you told us you slipped. Good job."

"Good job, Myra," they all said.

"You need to do an assignment about your mother. I want you to write her a letter and read it to us."

"What do I say?"

"That's up to you," Rachel said. "Just sit alone for a while and think about her. Don't you have a Winnie the Pooh? Hold it. Rock it. Let yourself go into a trance. Hug yourself. Mothers are a big loss." She stared into the middle of the circle. "Then write."

***

After group, Myra begged Grace for permission to call Keen, the urge to confess overwhelming.

"I drank, Dad." She sat at a small desk in a corner of the nurses' station and rubbed her hand on the polished surface. Tiny individual curls of dust rested on the pretend wood.

"You what?"

"When I was home. Saturday night. I left Nancy's and drank."

"I see," he said.

"I regret it," she said. "I'm going to work my program harder. I'm going to stay sober. I'm sorry."

When Myra had been eight, home from school with a bad cold, Keen had tucked her in for a nap and then left to go teach. He never missed a class. She lay in bed but couldn't fall asleep. How could anyone? Naps made no sense, all that light outside coming in. She sneezed and sneezed and her breathing got tight, a squeeze in her chest like the walls in the *Star Wars* trash compactor, secret monster buried. She was alone and she saw herself in her bedroom upstairs, the house silent and huge beneath her. The heat whooshed on and the furnace creaked, and Myra ran to the phone on the hallway table and dialed her father's office number at Kirkwood. When there was no answer, she called the main number and cried and asked the woman to please get her dad and tell him to come home because she couldn't breathe.

"He left you alone?" the switchboard operator asked.

"Please go get him," Myra said.

"Okay, honey; don't worry. We will. Hold on a minute."

When she came back and said he was on his way, she hung up and sat on the floor beneath her bedroom window and put her nose against the cold glass and watched the shape of her exhalations until he pulled up in the driveway. She ran downstairs.

"You all right?" He was at the side door, the one they used most of the time, his hand on the knob. The glare of the snow behind him made Myra squint. Keen rarely shoveled the sidewalks; they let their feet make paths that eventually set into place.

"I can't breathe."

He looked at her strangely, as if she had eaten a forbidden cookie, the giant tree behind him without leaves, bare branches reaching. "You seem to be breathing just fine."

"No," she said. She forced herself to cough. "It's still bad." She coughed again.

"I ended my lecture right in the middle."

Myra blinked, sniffled, her bangs in her eyes, Winnie the Pooh in the bend of her elbow.

"Okay." Keen sighed. "Let's give you some Robitussin."

"Dad?" Myra said into the phone. This one was dial-up, without buttons. This way no one could click into other conversations.

"I'm here," he said.

"I'm really, really sorry."

"Well, all right."

Should she say it? Yes. Because what would he say back? "I just have to find God's will for me." Myra grabbed a strand of hair but not hard enough to remove it, skin at the follicles pulled into a minuscule hill. She ran her finger over the bump.

"I see." Silence. She let it go on. Why didn't he say something? Ever? Grace reached over Myra's head for a blood pressure sleeve in a basket mounted to the wall. "Time's up," she whispered.

"You there, Dad?"

"You looking forward to coming home?" he asked.

"I have to go," Myra said. She spoke quietly, directly into the receiver, aware of Grace standing there to make sure she would do the right thing.

Sendoffs

Margaret stood in front of the whiteboard-on-wheels, her body covering some words on the list she had written in blue marker behind her, words they had all copied into their notebooks. *Friends. Spirituality. Family. Education. Being healthy.*

"Which one is most important?" Margaret asked.

"Spirituality," said Jen. "If you don't have God, you don't have anything."

"Family," said Bryan.

"Education," said Theresa. "I need to care about school."

"Being healthy," Myra said.

"Yes!" said Margaret, circling the word. "And for all of you, this means—" she wrote, at the top of the list, where she had left a space: SOBRIETY.

"When you start drinking and using, you…"

USE TO FEEL GOOD.

"Don't you?" she asked. They all nodded.

Yesterday, Bryan said he had seen down Margaret's blouse and gotten a glimpse of her nipple. She was so flat she didn't wear a bra. Teeny weeny.

"But once you become addicted, you…" She erased GOOD. USE TO FEEL.

The week before, Bliss had taken Myra and a few others to an AA meeting in the basement of the hospital—a small gymnasium with folding chairs in a circle right in the center. Several of the attendees had introduced themselves with a list.

"I'm Sandy and I'm an alcoholic, addict, and schizophrenic. I pass." Stonewashed jeans, strange and ill-fitting sweater, broad smile.

"Hi, I'm Jack and I'm an alcoholic, a food addict, and a manic-depressive. I had three years yesterday! I am so grateful for this life. It's all because of Alcoholics Anonymous. That's all." Chubby, balding, a wrinkly suit without a tie.

"Hi, I'm Katherine and I'm an alcoholic and a co-dependent." Sleeveless top, long blond hair. "When I was a child, my father raped me while my mother held me down and told me to be still." Myra saw a dark room, a large house, figures in shadow on the floor. Wondered how and why and where. Felt mentally deficient. She sat beside Myra, so Myra was blushing and hoped no one would notice.

"I'm still having nightmares," she said, looking at her lap. Her nails were manicured and polished a light brown. "I'm sorry. I shouldn't have said that. I have got to stop telling everybody everything. I think that's why I drink sometimes. Oh my God." An empty stage loomed behind her. Dim lights. "I pass."

It was Myra's turn.

"I'm Myra," she said. She was still thinking about the shadowed house but smiled. "I'm an alcoholic and an addict." Wasn't she? If she used a drug, wouldn't she become addicted to it, and therefore wasn't she already an addict? For her the term was pre-emptive. And Jen had said this was true.

"I'm so grateful to be sober." Was she? She didn't know.

"I'll pass," Myra said.

"Do you all use to feel?" Margaret asked. "Raise your hand if you know what I'm talking about. Anyone want to explain?"

"I was stoned all the time," Jen said. "I came to breakfast stoned. I didn't feel anything. All I thought about was getting stoned."

Was alcohol all Myra thought about? No. Not at all. Sometimes. Probably a lot more than she thought. She was probably obsessed with it and never realized the truth.

Theresa, who sat beside Myra, was nodding. She and Lisa were on Day Fifty-seven. Almost gone.

After class, everyone changed clothes and Margaret led them to the gymnasium for fitness stations: jumping jacks, sit-ups, deep knee bends, burpees, weights, exercise bikes.

"Are you scared?" Myra asked Theresa as they stood together, doing arm curls with tiny barbells.

"My mom said she quit, but I know she's lying," said Theresa. "They said no to halfway. I begged. So did Rachel." Myra was starting to like exercise. If it wasn't sports, it made her feel strong, capable. "And I know my brother still smokes weed." Margaret blew the whistle. "But they believe everything he says."

"You can do it," said Myra.

"I'll go to lock-up if I don't," said Theresa. Myra pictured patients in straight jackets, their arms tied to bedposts like Dixie on *All My Children*, like all those women on soap operas who got committed by evil men who wanted to control them.

Theresa put her hand over her eyes and started to cry. "Shit. I don't want to leave."

Myra hugged Theresa.

"God will look out for you," she said. "I know He will. I just know it." And she held Theresa hard and felt that what she said was true.

Theresa had already written goodbye in Myra's *Big Book*:

> You are a really neat & sweet girl. When u first came in u were having so many pity parties I thought I was gonna slap u!!!! You were also a bitch & wouldn't let anyone get to know u. I'm really glad u let us in. For sure we'll keep in touch. I wish I didn't have to go, but I guess I don't have much of a choice. Hope you stay sober!!!! Love ya, Theresa Nuezil.

"You okay over there?" Margaret called. The other patients stood at their stations and faced the center of the gym, two fingers on pulse points to determine their heart rate.

"I want to stay here," Theresa said, hugging Myra back, leaning into her. Tears dripped onto Myra's shoulder. "Where it's safe."

***

Abbey and Mitch had sex, and the smoke room was hushed with the news. Patients clustered together in twos and threes, flicking cigarettes into the black plastic ashtrays on the table. Jen was crying because of what they had done to the Community. She was on Day Fifty-four.

Myra felt the loss, too, but mildly, as if a distant friend told her that her grandmother had died.

"How?" Myra asked.

"They snuck into the kitchenette," Jen said. She used the butt of her Marlboro Red to light the next one.

They did it standing up? Myra didn't ask. There wasn't enough floor in the kitchenette for them to have done it any other way. Mitch was big, his chest muscular from football, and Abbey so small. They must have done it on the counter, like in *Fatal Attraction*. Myra pictured Mitch's hands squeeze what flesh they could find and settle on her nipples, unzip her jeans, slip his fingers into her underwear. Abbey taking fitful breaths in an effort to be quiet, her back crushed between Mitch and the counter.

Jen sniffled. "Mitch I can see, I guess."

"He was getting better, though," Myra said. He had shared in Community a lot: admitted he was addicted to pot, that he had always broken the fitness pledge and used during football season, that he had cheated on his girlfriend of two years so many times, that he had called his mom a worthless bitch. And after he grabbed Myra's ass during a hug, he apologized and hadn't done it since.

"Maybe," said Jen. "But Abbey was just fooling us! I can't believe her."

Jen repeated those words to Abbey in a special Community that Bliss called before afternoon group. Mitch and Abbey were both wearing pajamas—punishment—and they would leave Our Primary Purpose as soon as Community was over. They'd been expelled. Having sex on the unit had crossed a line, Bliss told them. Their parents were on their way.

Didn't they need to stay? Myra didn't ask. Abbey did. Abbey really, really needed to stay.

"Man, Mitch," Ron said, shaking his head from his chair in the circle. "I had faith in you." Abbey was grinning, just a little. Myra felt the patients' anger, the Community's anger—it hovered over their circle like a swarm. Ron looked at Abbey. "You think this is funny?"

"No," Abbey said. But her grin persisted, and Myra saw the Abbey from before her Own Up. She had returned. Had she ever left? Abbey thought they were a joke. She was amused.

There is nothing funny here, Myra didn't say. We are all working so hard. We need to be here. We need each other because of all that has happened to us. Whose fault was this, anyway? Weren't they only teenagers? Half of them weren't old enough to drive; two of them weren't old enough to have part-time jobs after school; none of them were old enough to vote. But their destinies were behind them, not before them. They would conquer nothing.

Lori glared from Abbey to Mitch and back again. "I had faith in you, too." She sat beside Ron. Study carrels lined the wall behind them. "I've seen you grow so much and now I think it was all a lie!" She started to cry. Ron started to cry. Jen pulled another Kleenex from her jeans pocket. Bryan started to cry.

Bliss said nothing while over her shoulder the kitchenette loomed. Myra looked into it, the ceiling light spilling onto the counter. The long tables where they ate meals were folded up and propped neatly against one wall. It was Monday. Pot roast for dinner.

Mitch looked at the carpet. "I'm sorry, man," he said.

"You're a piece of shit," Victor said, shaking his head.

Abbey's grin had shrunk. What would she do now? What would happen to her? Would she use cocaine again? What would her father do? Community closed with the Serenity Prayer, and Myra walked immediately to Abbey. She stood by the window.

"I wish you wouldn't have done that," Myra said. But she meant it, and it wasn't angry.

"Me, too, I guess," said Abbey.

"Please stay sober."

"I will," Abbey said. "I mean… I'll try." Abbey looked out at the river. The sky was solid gray and bare.

***

The Community was crying. Jen could barely tell Lisa and Theresa how much they had helped her. "You know," she said. "You know."

Bryan sniffled and let the tears drip.

"You gave me so many positive strokes," Victor said.

"You are a beautiful person," said Ron to Lisa. He didn't pray, but he clasped his hands and shook them a little as he spoke, like a preacher trying to convince a congregation. His words came slowly. "I will miss you both so much. Go to meetings." He was on Day Forty-four.

Lori was crying, too. "I'll miss your smile," she said to Lisa. Myra loved Lisa's giant dimples.

Myra,

    I'm glad you're working your program I kinda had doubts at first but I now I know you can do it. I'm going to miss you alot you're special you've helped me out alot. I love you alot. Write me—I'll send you the address whenever I get it. Stay sober!!! Hugs not drugs!!!! --Lisa Abernathy

"I'm scared, but I have God," Lisa had told Myra the night before as they were brushing their teeth.

"How long are you in halfway?" Myra spat Crest into the sink.

"Two years. Then I'll be in a foster family."

"Wow."

"I never have to go home again," she said. "Never."

"Please, please stay sober," Myra said to Lisa when it was her turn. She was leading this important Community, Theresa's and Lisa's last. Bliss watched from outside the circle, her face weathered but so pretty. When she smiled, rare as it was, you could spot a missing molar, graying canines. Bliss had been through hell, Jen said. How did Jen know everyone's stories?

Myra looked around the circle. "And I have an issue. I didn't stay sober when I went home," she said. There were new patients and very new patients, two in pajamas, but the Community was small. Only fifteen. It will fill up again, Rachel had said when Myra asked about it. It always does.

"And it hurt my recovery," Myra said. "A lot." Had it? She had apologized to Keen. She had confessed. Did it still hurt her?

"You know it did," she said. "It distracted me from my primary purpose, you know?" Was that true? Sure. But what was her primary purpose? God. It was God. It was Him. She felt the glee and saw herself atop a tower. Allowed it all in.

"But I know you'll both stay sober," Myra continued. "I'm praying for you. Our Community won't be the same." This was true. The Community would change. Myra would be a senior patient, the second oldest. They would look to her for wisdom and then she would leave, too, walk into The Outs a different girl. She was already different, wasn't she? Praying, reading, trying to keep from thinking about the wrong things. But who would she be without these tight daily routines, delivered meals, thick windows? In OPP time felt geologic, like plates were shifting or stars were dying or rocks were forming. One hour, one minute, one second inched so slowly into the next that Myra wondered how anyone survived the pace or survived without it.

Mom

Myra wrote how the Baby Magic had disappeared, that round pink bottle of lotion that smelled so thick and sweet it confused her. Candy. No—flowers. No—perfume. She wrote how Melanie had rubbed that lotion into her hands so often it was weird. How Melanie had sat on the edge of her bed. "Want to hear a lullaby?" And even when Myra had felt indifferent at those moments in time she had said yes, and she was glad and grateful because when she recalled those moments in time she felt not at all indifferent or bored but desperate for her mother. So her indifference felt like an illusion, almost a lie, as if it had existed but never existed. Feelings are deception. Feelings are betrayal.

    Myra did not write this. She wrote how Melanie had sung "The Streets of Laredo," a depressing song about a cowboy in a valley and death, while they lived in the middle of Iowa and were alive. Weird again. But Melanie was always in tune, and she circled her lips around the long *o* as if she were in deep concentration, and the tone of her voice vibrated gently in the air of the bedroom, and the glow of the nightlight warmed the walls up to the ceiling. The valley death song was what Myra expected and her mother had been right there in her flesh when it was cold and Myra was covered in blankets or when it was hot and Myra was clammy beneath only a sheet because they did not have air conditioning. Not then. She remembered her parents talking about it, the sounds of serious discussion.

Myra wrote how she had sat in Melanie's lap, but only sometimes. She told Myra once to get off. Get off, please. And Myra had never known why this was, why she had not sat in her mother's lap a whole lot more, and why at that particular moment she had to get off. Melanie's voice clear and firm.

What had she done? she didn't write. Was this why prayer never worked?

She remembered driving with Melanie every afternoon at one o'clock to daycare and hating that she left Myra there. For nap, the children used mats on the floor that were not soft, and it was broad daylight so nap didn't make sense anyway. Stupid. And all Myra could think about was her mother. And when she would come back. She had never been like the other children, whom the care providers interrupted—*Time to put your stuff away! Your mom's here!* Myra knew how to tell time. At three-fifty, ten minutes until Melanie's return, Myra screwed the top onto her jar of paste, and picked up all the bits and pieces of leftover construction paper and put them in the trash, and put her scissors and crayons in the correct coffee mugs, and pulled her hat to her ears and buttoned her coat and waited in her miniature chair at the table, her fingers wrapped around the drawstrings of her cloth bag. Sometimes her nose ran and she wiped the snot onto her mitten. Myra waited for her mother in silence, a different silence than when she died. That silence had blipped itself into existence and grown, little by little, a shadow of quiet and gentle doom. Myra hadn't realized this was happening, her spirit being hushed. Her soul. Did she have a soul? Did anyone? Was it really in there? Myra thought so, now. Or was she just telling herself that souls existed, like everything else?

She wrote how the daycare people did not like her departure routine, but that she kept doing it, so they eventually gave in. Let it go. Let her do what she wanted. "You getting ready for your mom?" they would ask, and Myra nodded. But when Melanie showed up, Myra did not run to her and hug her knees. She got out of her chair and walked over to you and stood beside you as the other children glued and painted and crayoned and the grown-ups reached down to help them. Myra looked at them all as if to say, Here she is. My mother has her hand on my shoulder, and this is how it is supposed to be, this is the world, my mother beside me, filling up all the space there ever was. Ready to take me home.

***

Myra folded in half the pieces of paper she had written her letter on. Three sides full, single-spaced, with a few sentences on the fourth.

"I couldn't think of anything else." Myra looked up.

Jen and Lori and Stephanie were crying. The other two patients were new: Jeanie with the curly hair, drug of choice pot, still in pajamas; Noelle with her arm in a cast, drug of choice speed, newly dressed. Noelle's lips were trembling, and Jeanie was looking at the ceiling.

"Good job, Myra," said Rachel. "I think you needed to get that out." She cleared her throat. "Do we have any feedback?"

"I love you so much," Jen sniffled.

"Theresa would have been proud of you," said Stephanie. "That's the truest thing you've ever said."

"It made me miss my mom," said Lori. She sobbed.

"Are you okay?" asked Myra.

"No," said Lori. "Fuck!" She wiped her nose with her palm. Two tears dripped from her jaw to her collarbone. "Can I please have a Kleenex?"

Rachel shook her head. "You need to feel those tears. Myra," she looked right at her. "You never dealt with your mother's death. I think you know that now."

And how should she have done that? No one had given her directions. Was there a map?

"She will always be there. And you need to feel her, not drink her away. You need to let yourself mourn. Do you understand?"

What about my dad? Myra didn't ask. He's never *stopped* feeling her. She was a curse. A Baby Magic spell.

"I get it," Myra said.

"I don't think you do," said Rachel. "I'll say it again. You have never dealt with your mother's death. And you cannot drink it away. Do you agree?"

"Yes."

"Why?"

"I don't know."

"Have a think," said Rachel. "We'll wait."

"I don't need one," Myra knew exactly what to say. "Because when I miss her, I drink." Not true.

"What else do you do?"

"I pull out my hair." That wasn't true, either. And she didn't pull her hair out anymore.

"And?"

"I don't know."

Rachel shook her head. "Until you're willing, Myra, you're going to struggle around this. Remember willingness."

"What does that mean?"

"To get better, you have to be willing to feel pain. To work the program around your issue."

"And if you don't, you have to at least want to want to," said Jen.

"That's right," said Rachel.

"I do," said Myra.

"I don't think you're there yet," said Rachel.

"Yes, I am," said Myra.

"We're recommending counseling after you're out," said Rachel. "We've already talked to Keen about it."

"Okay," she said.

"You're better, Myra," said Rachel. "But you are not well. You still have a lot of work to do."

"I know."

"No, she doesn't," said Lori. "She doesn't know anything."

"Why do you say that?" asked Rachel.

"She didn't even cry when she read that letter."

She hadn't cried as she wrote it, either. And she had tried. Hard. Holding Winnie the Pooh, tracing the frayed felt lines of his mouth and nose, rocking on the edge of her bed. She even held herself. But tears would not come, and Myra did not know why this was. Didn't people cry when their mother died? She had once—or had that been about something else? In therapy you never knew if you were really feeling something or if it was just reactionary. Everything you felt was always in doubt. Myra had written that letter from her desk chair in her room, taken breaks and stared into the frosted glass window over the sink and felt despair. She felt it now, too, but it was changing into space between Myra and all of them, as if she were walking away, building the distance and leaving them there in an unfinished circle until she disappeared.

Artifice

During their last chapters of treatment, patients with over forty days went to a Youth AA meeting on Thursdays. Before Charlie had graduated, the night of his last Community, he had told Myra he would be there. He'd spoken from behind her, after dinner as Myra stood at the tray stand. He had just folded up one of the tables.

"Every Thursday," Charlie said. "You'll see me."

Myra turned around. Patients were filing out of the dining room. He looked right at her for the first time in weeks. He had a crumple in his lips when he held them together, an acne mark on his left temple. He held an unlit cigarette. No techs in sight.

She kissed him, leaned in hard and fast, then pulled back. He looked stunned, grabbed her hand, squeezed it, walked quickly to the smoke room.

That night Myra put her hand on her vagina, cupped it around the precious flesh over her pubic bone, the abrasive hair. She squeezed, ventured her fingers inside and moved them until she came, her face in the pillow. She did it again. She wanted a cigarette. Did other girls masturbate in OPP? At all? Why hadn't she done this sooner? Of course boys did it since they always wanted sex, since they always tried to convince girls to do it. Girls were never the ones on no-sex contracts.

But Jen had sworn it off since all the counselors and techs warned patients: no sex or relationships in your first year of sobriety. You have to concentrate on recovery. The phone numbers she had gotten at Youth AA from boys were totally platonic, she said.

"I got so many. Look." She held her cigarette in one hand and with her other showed Myra her tiny black address book with gold, alphabetical category letters down the fore-edge and Our Primary Purpose emblazoned in gold on the front. "My mom ordered it for me. It fits in my pocket so I can take it everywhere, whether I have a purse or not."

Did they all want to give you their numbers? Myra didn't ask. Or did they have to since it was AA? Myra stared at the address book and realized that she could start friendships with anybody. No one in the program would turn someone away.

"I wish I lived here," Myra said.

Jen set her cigarette in the U of the ashtray and hugged Myra. They left their arms around each other's shoulders. Myra saw the lines in the floor where tiles came together.

"I do, too. You'll come visit me all the time though, right?"

"Sure," said Myra. Were there sober teenagers in Iowa City? She hadn't seen any at the meeting she went to.

"I met Bliss's daughter," said Jen. "Her name's Charity. She's been sober nine months. She is *so* pretty. Her other daughter is in the program, too, but I haven't seen her yet."

Myra knew it ran in families. This awful disease. She saw Charity and Bliss, yelling and then making up and going to a meeting together.

"Did you see Charlie?"

"Yep." Jen had become okay with Myra's feelings for Charlie. She couldn't help how she felt, Myra had explained. You can help what you do, though, Jen had said. I know, Myra had said. I'm sorry. I shouldn't have run. I regret it.

Lie.

"What did he say?" Myra asked.

"That he'll be there next week for sure."

***

Myra had wanted to sit against the wall, but Jen insisted they sit at the table, which stretched fully across most of the long, windowless room. So many teenagers. Most of them were smoking. Feathered hair. A few mohawks. Barrettes. Makeup. Acid-washed jeans. Cropped jeans. Jean jackets. Shorts. Pin-striped shorts with white belts. T-shirts: Led Zeppelin, Metallica, Michael Jackson, Prince, Joan Jett, The Violent Femmes. Pink and purple Izods. Plaid Polos. Canvas Tretorns, plastic jellies (wasn't that plastic?). Top Siders. Penny loafers. Flip-flops. The walls of the room were brown, half paneled and half spackled. The carpet was brown and thin, the chairs mismatched metal or wood. AA slogans were framed and hung in different places, just like in Iowa City: One Day at a Time, Easy Does It, Keep it Simple. Let Go and Let God. Take What You Like and Leave the Rest.

Charlie showed up a few minutes after the meeting started, took a seat along the wall, saw Myra, and beamed. Huge and loving. She would do anything for him. Slide into his pocket. Follow him around. Hug him and never let go. Beg him to stay with her forever. Seal him in.

Myra had felt the same way about Mark. After she spent the night with him in the park shelter, Keen had grounded her, but he allowed Mark to come over. He brought her a spaghetti dinner in

Tupperware, a red rose. He called her every day. With someone loving her so much, how could she keep from being eager? From becoming afraid he would leave? Because he would, wouldn't he?

"You are co-dependent," Rachel said. Myra finally shared about Mark, about how she had adored him and how he dumped her, how afterward she had slashed at her wrists.

"You are afraid everyone will abandon you," said Rachel.

"So am I," said Lori.

"Me, too," said Jen.

"Probably because of your mother," said Rachel.

"And since you want to control people, you're manipulative," said Jen.

I have to keep them close, Myra didn't say. I can't let them get away.

Mark had loved her at first. He took her to Homecoming. She had been his escort down the aisle during the Homecoming nomination ceremony in the auditorium. The whole school knew who she was after that. They were a couple. Myra walked down the halls of City High as Mark Ahrens's girlfriend, visible and safe at the same time.

"You have to focus on yourself," said Lori.

But I think about myself all the time, Myra didn't say. I make myself sick.

They had a song, one that Mark picked for them. They were parked on the street in front of Myra's house; he was dropping her off after they had dry-humped on his basement sofa until he came. Their routine. He lay on top of her and they made out wildly and moved together as if having sex. Myra loved it but they always stopped abruptly, as soon as Mark slowed down and stopped moving and then got up and used the bathroom while Myra reconstituted herself and sat in her own wet, crossing her legs, hoping her underwear would absorb it all. The first few times, Myra had not understood why he thrust so hard and then quit, but she didn't dare ask him, didn't dare risk his affection by bringing up anything physical or gross, anything having to do with fluid.

He reached across the space between the bucket seats and took her hand. The motor ran softly, the windows down, the night quiet, and Mark put his hand on the back of her neck like men did on soap operas, as if he'd been practicing. He pulled her to him and kissed her as the radio played "You Are So Beautiful to Me" by Joe Cocker.

"You remember me telling you that?" he asked.

Myra nodded from her star of happiness and felt like she was looking down on the planet. He kissed her cheek.

But a few months after the Homecoming dance, after New Year's Eve, he started calling less. He stopped wanting to make out as often, stopped meeting her at her locker after every class period—only after lunch, and sometimes it seemed like he didn't want to be there. He stopped putting his arm around her in the hallway, claiming her. They didn't dry hump every time they went out, and whenever they didn't, Myra worried. She wanted to fix whatever was wrong. Claw at something.

"Co-dependents are people pleasers," said Rachel, her hands folded neatly in her lap. She had new shoes. Black flats. "They're very afraid. Pleasing others or becoming obsessed with people is how they survive."

Survive what? Myra didn't say.

Mark's slow rejection had started when Myra took him to the University of Iowa museum. She knew it had.

"My mom used to work here," she said as they parked and got out of his Trans Am.

She liked sculptures and paintings but also the museum itself, the grand staircase in the center, the shining floors. The basement had always been Myra's favorite place—she remembered Melanie leading her there and waiting as Myra pretended to study the permanent exhibits from Africa and Egypt but loved mostly the space itself. Boxy rooms and statues resting on pedestals, display cases shining, corners sharp. White walls with miniature statues balanced on square shelves, their shadows slanted. Soft spotlights from the ceiling and hallways that led to rooms you didn't expect.

"You like it here?" Mark asked. He was wearing his football jacket. They stood before a painting thick with color, a boat on a pond and a child sitting alone. "Why?"

"It's just so nice here. It's… like… beautiful, you know?"

He stared at the painting. "I hate art."

"We don't have to stay."

"Good. Let's go to the mall after this."

But after the mall, they hadn't gone to his basement. They had barely even kissed. That afternoon had been the benchmark, the milestone, the before and after of Myra's constant panic. When they were together, she tamped it down so Mark wouldn't notice; when they weren't together, when Myra was home in her room wondering why he hadn't called—or right after he had called but sounded distracted, bored with her—she tried to purge the panic from her mind by letting it out. Sometimes the sorrow came immediately and she sobbed. But if she couldn't dredge up enough fear she would play on her tape recorder "You Are So Beautiful to Me" (she had recorded it from the radio), lie on her bedroom carpet, curl into the fetal position, and think about losing him, about how empty she would be, until she started crying.

Because wouldn't forcing emotion help it go away? If you cried, wouldn't the sorrow and terror get smaller?

Mark broke up with her at Señor Pablos, a Mexican restaurant that used orange cheese in all its entrées and served her a lukewarm tostada.

"I just want to be friends," he said. They sat at a tiny, two-person table with a picture of a Sombrero as a centerpiece. Myra started to cry. Mark looked like he wanted to hide her under the table and leave.

"Why?"

"I don't know. I just think we should only be friends."

"Let's just… give it another try," she sobbed. A little girl watched them from her highchair. "Please?"

That was who Myra had been, the girl who begged. The girl who, when Mark had dropped her off at home, had opened a kitchen drawer while her father was sleeping and taken out the paring knife that could barely cut through the skin of an apple, carried it upstairs to her room, the metal handle warming in her grip, and slashed her wrists with it, just enough to draw blood that dripped into the colors of the carpet.

Because what else was there to do? Sit on her bed in all the desperate?

Keen found her, grabbed her, rushed her to the car. He said later he didn't know why he went upstairs. He just felt something. (And hadn't that been God? Taking care of her? Zapping her father into awareness, pushing him up the stairs? Wasn't she blessed?) He took her to the emergency room and they admitted her, woozy and vacant, tiny strips of adhesive closing the cuts on her wrists. She was glad to be removed, tucked away into a room where no one could see her, no roommate, the television loud, packets of round graham crackers and pints of milk in the nurses' station she could go get any time she wanted while she adapted to Elavil, while a psychiatrist assessed her, a tall jolly man with a shaggy beard and rimless glasses.

"We'll get you feeling better," he said after they met for the first time. She believed him. She felt hope.

Keen visited her for one hour every day when he was done teaching.

"I brought you some Saltines," he said the first day. Was he crying? Was he about to? Myra couldn't tell. He looked unnatural, afraid.

"They have some in the nurses' station," she said. "I don't need them."

"I brought you your favorite books," he said the next day. Judy Blume, Paula Danziger. Creased and worn, paintings of pretty teenagers on the covers. The characters were sad kids trying, like Myra.

But they weren't debacles in hospitals.

"Reading's too weird," she said. Words on pages were like weights anyway—when she tried to read she felt like dropping to the ground. "I can't."

"I'll just sit with you awhile."

An After School Special was on about a kid whose friend killed himself. They sat in silence.

Why didn't he ask how she was? Why didn't he ever ask how she was?

After he left, she turned off the television and listened to "Bad" and "With or Without You" over and over on her tape recorder. She pulled a chair to the window and looked at the vast, flat, gravel rooftops of Mercy Hospital, black and brick chimneys disappearing into night as the sun set.

The medication would work soon, the doctor said. Don't worry.

When she went back to school a week later, she was the girl who tried to kill herself. The girl who went to the hospital for a week. The girl who had a psychiatrist. The girl who was taking medication for *depression*. What? What was that, anyway? The girl who Mark had dumped. The unstable girl.

"Screw them," said Nancy. "Who cares, sweetie?"

Myra did. She always had.

Not anymore. Myra lit a cigarette, looked around the room at all the teenagers in recovery. They would be her friends. She would not need so much. She would care less. Charlie smiled at her. She smiled back but asked God to help her not focus on Charlie and pay attention. Listen. Stay in the moment.

***

After the meeting, Charlie smoothed the back of her hair, which was down in back, the sides up and held with only two barrettes. Her patches had filled in. He hugged her.

"I miss you," Charlie said.

"I miss you, too," Myra said.

"It's weird out here," Charlie said. "You see how fucked up everyone else is. It's hard."

We could be together out here, Myra didn't say. I live in Iowa City, and you live in Des Moines. They're only two hours apart. We could have a long-distance relationship.

They walked outside, where groups were forming, congregating around the entrance and the side of the building that was covered in flyers of all colors and kinds.

"Who drove you?"

"Travis," Myra said. Travis the tech, a rotund man with steel-rimmed glasses and a hearty laugh. He was leaning against their van at the curb. Tiny bits of trash littered the gutter—you could only notice if you looked.

"Five minutes!" Travis called.

"What if he tells them I talked to you?" Myra asked.

"You're on The Outs. You get to talk to who you want."

"Anyone have a name that starts with Z?" Jen yelled. Two hands went up and she ran over. "I want every line filled!"

Two girls standing beside them rolled their eyes, purses over their shoulders. One of them had a ponytail and held a pamphlet called *Is A.A. For Me?* The other had thick black hair down to her waist and clear white skin and large dark eyes. She was beautiful.

"Myra, this is Charity," Charlie said. "She's Bliss's daughter."

"Oh wow," said Myra.

"That's me," she said. "Nice to meet you."

"You, too," Myra said.

"Can I get your number?" Charlie asked.

"Sure. We can go to a meeting sometime. You ever been to the one on South First?" She pulled a pen from her purse and wrote her number on a memo pad, then tore off the sheet for Charlie.

This was nothing, Myra told herself. This was okay in AA. Boys got girls' numbers all the time. Girls got boys' numbers all the time. And if he wanted to date Charity, Charlie wouldn't ask for her number right in front of Myra. Would he? What were the rules? Were teenagers actual couples in AA? Or did everyone just have sex with everyone else?

"Hey, Charity!" Jen came bounding over.

"Hey," Charity smiled.

"I graduate next week," Jen said. "Can I get your number? Want to go to a meeting?"

"Sure," Charity said, writing it on her pad. The girl beside her looked away, as if she were reading something on the bulletin board.

"Your mom is like totally amazing."

"Oh. Yeah."

"Time to go!" Travis called.

"Come on, Myra," said Jen. She walked toward the van.

"Hold on," called Charlie. He grabbed Myra and hugged her again. "Write to me, okay? I can't come next week. I have to go out with my parents. I love you. You can do it."

Please be my boyfriend, she didn't say. Please mean I love you in a way that I know you don't.

"I love you, too," she said calmly into his ear.

Charlie let her go, and Myra climbed into the van. On the way back to the unit, she looked out the window as Jen talked to everyone about the glories of recovery.

Morals

During her final Community, Jen had sobbed. Three times Stephanie held out the blue hospital box of Kleenex, but Jen held up her hand, snot rivering down her upper lip, curving into her mouth. "No. I need to fully feel these tears." She cried so hard that she could say no more than how much she would miss everyone, how grateful she was, how they could never understand how much she loved them. Myra had never seen anyone cry with such little inhibition, such a hurling of appearances into the wind.

She never wanted to be like that.

Afterward, as they sat in the smoke room, Jen watched Myra read her goodbye.

Dear Myra,
    You've made so much progress here. You've been thru a lot. But I know you can work thru it all on your way to a very <u>happy</u> sobriety. It'll be hard but the pay-offs are immeasurable. Remember, it's ok to be selfish in this program and also remember, you can't give away what you don't have. Get it for yourself and then begin to share of yourself. Just remember that God sets the time schedule not U. You can't do and feel everything at once—you have to

take it as He gives it to you. And He'll never give you more than U can handle, so if He doesn't give it to you it must mean you're not ready 4 it. God loves you, so let Him. He will save you from yourself. Remember, you'll still have lots of problems but now you can deal with them sanely and you don't have to hide behind a smile, a pity pot, or a beer bottle! It's important for you to know people can be happy, have fun, <u>and</u> be sober. You are an alcoholic and you are a drug addict. But the fact that I love you (and everyone) means that you are an OK person and you are worth being loved. It's really OK to love yourself. You deserve It!!! I LOVE YOU 4-EVER—Jen Harrison.

Jen had an even longer P.S.: Her entire goodbye started on the final page of "Growing Up All Over Again," continued through the margins of "Unto the Second Generation," and finally curved around the title of the chapter "*Me* an Alcoholic?"

"I love you," Jen said.

"I love you, too," Myra said. "This is beautiful." She tried to bring up tears, to feel the power of Jen's words. But she couldn't.

"It goes on for five pages." Jen's hands were shaking. The red in her face splotched without pattern over her freckles, down her neck.

"I know. Thank you."

Jen wiped the palm of her hand on the leg of her jeans. "My mom took off somewhere."

"Why?"

"I think it just happened. So I don't know." She sniffled. "So my dad moved into the house. He's picking me up tomorrow with Jeremy. It'll be the three of us."

"Where did she go?"

Jen shrugged. "She never cared, anyway."

"How old is your brother again?"

"Six years older. He is such an asshole."

"You have God," Myra said. "More than any of us." But a lot of other people don't, Myra didn't say. Did God help them anyway, or let them drift?

"I feel Him right now. I just have to let Him in. I just have to. Or I'm sunk."

They held hands while the other patients sang James Taylor in soft voices. They lit each other's cigarettes.

***

Myra sat at a study carrel and read her Fourth Step so far: her searching and fearless moral inventory. She was on Day Fifty-six. The *Big Book* had a structure for Step Four, with columns and categories patients could use. But it looked like something for much older people, who had been through marriage and employment and all the ruin and conflict they wrought.

I'm Resentful At	The Cause	Affects My
Mr. Brown	His attention to my wife. Told my wife of my mistress. Brown may get job at the office.	Sex relations Self-esteem. (fear) Sex relations. Self-esteem. (fear) Security. Self-esteem. (fear)

| My Wife | Misunderstands and nags. Likes Brown. Wants house put in her name. | Pride— Personal sex relations— Security (fear) |

That's it? That's all he had to write about having a mistress, about being jealous? A chart like this got rid of everything that was wrong with you? Myra could not wait.

But not everyone used the chart.

"Write down everything you've done wrong in your life," Rachel said. "Who you resent, sure, but also who you hurt and how." They were standing in Rachel's office at her desk right after Small Group. Myra held her legal pad to her chest.

But I haven't done that much wrong, Myra didn't say. I'm not like Bryan or Charlie or Abbey. I don't really hurt people.

But thinking this way was detrimental to recovery. Alcoholics weren't supposed to consider themselves unique.

"And wow," Jen had said before she left. "That was your problem when you got here! Nobody had it worse than you. You felt so sorry for yourself. You thought you had it so bad." It had been a Tuesday: French dip sandwiches. They sat across from each other. "You were on, like, the biggest pity pot ever."

But I was hurt, Myra didn't say. I ached inside. There was not a cavern in the world bigger than the one in my soul. How else could I have been?

"Oh, I know," Myra said. She rolled her orange on the table, pressing hard to loosen the skin before she peeled it off. Tiny bits of what looked like plastic coated her palm and left a fleeting streak on the surface of the table. Was that pesticide?

"You're not special and neither am I," said Jen.

Myra was afraid her Fourth Step would be shorter than anyone else's. A super short story, that's all she was. The longest one ever had been Cliff's, who graduated before Myra got there. He was a legend. Thirty-two lined notebook pages, single-spaced, back-to-back. And he was only fifteen.

"His Fifth Step took two whole days," Theresa had said. That had been a Wednesday. Meatloaf and mashed potatoes that tasted like sand. "He had to do it early so he could finish before he graduated."

"But he was super bad," Lisa had said. "You should just be honest, Myra."

"Make a list of people and write down the ways you've hurt each of them," said Rachel.

"Make columns, like in the *Big Book*," said Bliss. "Don't you know which page it's on?"

"What about how you've hurt yourself?" asked Erin. "Don't forget about how your drinking has hurt *you*, Myra."

"Just write your story," said Grace. "Don't hold back."

"Make a box with three columns," said Russell Dean. "Then fill them the fuck out."

"Try making a list with numbers," said Erin. "Everything you've done wrong, starting from your first memory."

1. Rocked my highchair back when I was two after my mom told me to stop. Hit my head on kitchen floor. Hurt my mother because I didn't listen. Hurt myself because I hit my head.
2. Jumped on my parents' bed while they were in the kitchen. I felt guilty. Hurt myself because I did something I felt guilty for.
3. Refused to use a bag for Halloween candy when I was six and carried it all in my hands. My dad had to pick

it all up behind me. Hurt my dad because he was angry. Hurt myself because I lost a lot of candy.
4. Played desk-up with girls in fourth grade when Mrs. Bronkhorst was substituting. We didn't stop, even when she begged, and she almost started crying. Hurt Mrs. Bronkhorst because we were mean to her for no reason. Hurt myself because I felt guilty about it. Hurt my dad when they called him at work and told him I was in the principal's office. My dad didn't need that.
5. Blamed myself for my mom's car accident. (Did I? I think I did.) Hurt myself because it wasn't my fault. My dad told me that, but I didn't listen. Hurt my dad because I didn't respect him.

If Myra had to go backward in time—if she missed something—she drew a V with the point between the two numbers, where it belonged in the order of events, and filled it in with tiny letters. Her legal pad pages stretched from edge to edge and corner to corner. The list became a skewed chronology. She jumped from place to place, time to time, wrong to wrong.

6. Slapped Eric Womack when he told me he didn't like my haircut. Hurt him because I slapped him. Hurt me because I wasn't strong enough to blow him off. I felt weak.
7. Played gymnastics with Harriet the Cat when I was four. Hurt the cat because she became scarred and weird.
8. Listened in on Dad's phone conversation with Mrs. Ronalds, the vice-principal, after I ran away in sixth grade. He said I was just trying to get attention. Hurt him because I betrayed trust (even though he didn't know—did I still hurt him?) Hurt me because I heard

something that was none of my business. I did want to get attention & it was hard to know that.

She pictured water washing away sand and dust on a stone tablet, a dig, an excavation. Was that release she felt as she wrote? She told herself it was. She told herself it would be even better after her Fifth Step—when you shared your Fourth Step with another person, told them the exact nature of your wrongs. The Fifth Step was when it all really got cleared away, cut down, removed. When everything changed.

***

Victor had disappeared, run away a third time. They all talked about it at dinner. No one got to say goodbye.

"All we can do is pray for him," said Jen.

"He's really, really bad," said Ron. "God damn it. This disease." He stared at his Salisbury steak with gravy and peas and got up from the table, put his tray in the cart, and started to cry. Lori got up and offered a hug, but Ron walked past her into the hallway.

"He's probably going to talk to Bliss," said Lori. Ron talked to Bliss a lot, one-on-one. Myra thought it was weird.

"So he's just gone?" asked Jeanie.

"Yep," said Sam.

"That's fucked up," she said.

"So is addiction," Sam said.

"Should we pray for him right now?" asked Jen. A few of them nodded and bowed their heads.

Please look out for Victor. Myra put her hands in her lap and squeezed them together. Please don't let him die. But did she really think he would? Were *jail, insanity, or death* really the only three fates for addicts without AA and God? She wasn't sure and felt like a liar and wondered if God would disqualify her or forgive her, on which end of His grace she fell. Neither felt right or correct.

    Please help him find the program. There, that was better. This she knew she really wanted, and it was selfless. Please help Victor stay alive, find You, find happiness. She slitted one eye open to see if the others were still praying. The dusky light from the windows shined on the tops of their heads.

Step Five

Myra was finished giving her Fifth Step to Erin. She hadn't cried and she didn't know why not. Erin and Myra got to use the conference room—the two of them sat at one end of that large table, the table where Keen learned all that Myra had done, that she pulled out her hair like Rochester's woman in the attic, like an institutionalized loony. Had he been devastated? He wasn't really that kind of parent. She saw that now. He wasn't involved and would not be involved. And her failures were out on the table, known and gone. She didn't own them anymore. The air did. God did.

And Erin did. She hadn't spoken much. That's not appropriate, Erin had said when they sat down. She was there to listen—that was her role—and Myra should not get upset if Erin didn't seem to react.

But on number thirty, Erin's eyes closed. Myra kept reading, and then Erin's chin dropped to her chest. Her glasses slid down and nearly fell into her lap before she jerked herself awake.

"Were you asleep?" Myra asked.

"No, not really. I'm just tired."

"Should we stop?"

"We can't. I… I worked last night and I haven't gone home yet. I should have rescheduled my shift for this." She took off her glasses and rubbed her eyes, shook out her hair. "That's better. Do you have a lot left?"

Myra felt punched.

"I don't know."

"I'm sorry, Myra. I'm here. You know I'm here."

> Myra,
> And God made woman. Sensitive, beautiful, loving. You are all those things.
> –Erin

Myra finished. She wanted that relief, that uplift, no matter what.

"Okay. Well." Erin went through her purse and pulled out a compact. She opened it and held the tiny mirror up to Myra. "Look at yourself," Erin said.

Myra saw her face, narrow with round cheeks. Her brown eyes the color of earth. She used to say to herself that they were the color of mud. How demeaning. How cruel.

"You don't ever have to drink again," Erin said. "You can have a choice."

"Okay," Myra said. She tried to hear that, pictured herself standing in the middle of a prairie, staying dry while rain poured around her.

"How do you feel?" Erin snapped the compact closed, stood up and stretched.

"Fine," Myra said.

"Do you feel any different?"

"Yeah," Myra said.

"Calmer, maybe?"

"Definitely."

"God is here," Erin said. "You've found Him. You've discovered Him."

Erin walked Myra back to the door of the unit and hugged her goodbye.

"Take care of yourself, okay?"

"I will," Myra said. She held up her legal pad. "What do I do with this?"

"I burned mine."

"Can you take it? I really don't want it anymore."

"I might get in trouble for that. Just burn it when you get home. Like a ceremony, out with the bad and in with the good."

"Okay."

Erin waited at the elevator. Myra entered the unit and let the door click to a close behind her. She didn't feel lighter. She didn't feel like a new girl. Had she let God in? She needed to work harder. She would keep her inventory. Because she should never forget how fucked up she was, how much there was to do.

Graduation

They took turns saying goodbye, going around the circle one at a time.

"I didn't get a chance to know you," said Pam with the Madonna bracelets, drug of choice heroin. She was on Day Two. "But I can tell that you're a really special person."

"You saved my life," said Ron, tears in his eyes. He had ten more days, then to halfway. He was better about praying. "I'll miss you so much."

"You've grown so much," said Sam. He was going home in fourteen days, folding right back into his family. Like Myra. But her family wasn't a family, so quiet, so few. "And you helped me a lot."

"Good luck," said Anne with the curly bangs, drug of choice speed. She was in her first week and she hated them.

"You've really grown and changed," said Lori. She still had to break up with her boyfriend who sold pot. She swore she would before she got out. "Especially since you got back from your run. I've learned a lot from you."

"I wish you the best," said Zack with a forehead scar, drug of choice speed. He stared at Myra's breasts a lot.

"Take care of yourself out there," said John with the mohawk, drug of choice downers. His favorite band was Bucket of Blood, but he was actually super nice.

"I don't know you, but I can tell how important you've been," said Millicent with the wild curly hair, drug of choice cocaine. She was on Day Four.

"The Community's going to be weird without you," said Stephanie. She was out in two days and couldn't wait to resume cheerleading. "I'm going to miss you so much."

"You really helped me," said Chad. "I love you. Thank you." He was going to halfway for the summer, then back home, where he would start high school in the fall.

For the last five minutes of anyone's final Community, techs and counselors who were there came in to close the ceremony.

"We'll miss you," said Grace. "You're a very special lady, and I think you're starting to realize how special you are."

"I've enjoyed working with you," said Margaret. "I've seen so many changes in you over the past two months! You're a winner, Myra. Keep up the good work."

Rachel was taking a day off. Myra didn't care.

It's been a Joy to work with you and struggle with your issues. Remember you don't have any problems that can't be improved on.

>You are starting a new life, one day at a time. Keep in touch. –Love, Rachel Winters

"You've done some good work," said Russell Dean. "Go to meetings."

Afterward, the newer patients went to the smoke room and all the older patients circled around Myra, waiting for hugs. A few of them were crying. Myra felt like an infant who didn't understand object permanence, that the room would remain after she left it, that people were still there when she no longer saw them, that rhythms continued when she could no longer hear them. She felt like her absence would leave an irreparable tear in the fabric, a permanent hole in the ceiling, a crack in the foundation that held up the house. She knew these feelings were wrong and prayed for God to remove her self-centeredness. But as she hugged and hugged and felt bodies loving her back, she wished that her presence mattered as much as she felt it did, that her perceptions were not a lie. Myra tried to find the spot between feeling and truth, that place that might be at the top of a mountain in beams of sunlight or at the shore of an ocean as waves unfurled on her toes or deep in a jungle as sounds of insects deafened her own voice. She knew serenity existed somewhere between right here and everywhere, but she did not know how anyone ever found it.

***

Keen did not come into the unit—parents were never allowed there—but instead met her in the conference room. She walked in carrying her suitcase, the one that had been her mother's. She had forgotten about it, a rectangle of history, scratches and broken lock and loose latch.

"You have a brand-new daughter," said Grace.

"I didn't want a new one," Keen said, hugging her. "Just a revised version." He held her by the shoulders at arms' length. "You look different."

"I am different," Myra said. "I'm sober."

"You're only two weeks sober, remember," Grace said. "That's a lot less than sixty days. You need to go to a meeting right away and get numbers. Find a sponsor."

"I know," said Myra. "I've got my plan. I'm going to a meeting tonight."

"We'd keep all of you longer if we could," said Grace.

"Blasted insurance," said Keen.

"Aren't they awful?" asked Grace. "Sixty days is nothing."

Myra became afraid.

"Bye, honey," Grace said. "Stay sober. Your life depends on it."

"I will." She hugged Grace, who wasn't all that bad.

Myra,

You are special to me. You are a loving and lovable person. You are strong. I wish you all good things. You will get them all because you are determined. Work your program and it will work for you. I love you! -Grace Goss

"Ready?" Keen asked.

No, Myra didn't say, hooking her thumb into the crook of her purse. Nancy's letters tucked into the outside pocket.

When they opened the doors to the parking lot, the sun was so bright it hurt her eyes. She felt a dull snap of pain in her forehead. Her desire to change almost burned her insides, glowed like fire contained in the trunk of an ancient tree. To not worry, to love herself. She looked at her father as he loaded her suitcase into a new car. He had finally given up on the Nova, he said. They still had it at home, but he had bought them a new Ford Escort, white with black trim.

"You like it? It starts every time," Keen said, smiling. Had Myra ever seen him happy? Was he relieved that she was out, that she was coming home? She loved him so much. Maybe now he would talk to her more. But no. She needed to let go. To stop wanting. Why was she still wanting so much? Isn't that what got her in OPP in the first place?

Keen pulled onto Interstate 80 and cornfields zipped by, the earth flat to the horizon line. The vanishing point—wasn't that what you aimed for when you were trying to draw? Had she learned that in art class last year? She had—she remembered. That had been a good moment in Myra's life—she'd been engrossed, learning and doing. Why hadn't she delved into drawing? Didn't she love art? What was wrong with her?

"Watch this," Keen said. He turned on the air conditioning. "Feel that!"

"Wow," Myra said. She lit a cigarette and cracked the window. Her father did the same.

She held her *Big Book* open in her lap, then closed it and studied the index patients had created along the fore-edge. One entry after another, ink always red, a name with the page number where Myra could find their goodbye. She started to read each one in order, long and short and meaningful and meaningless. She gazed out the window toward the landscape she recognized. The sky never has to end, and it's been here forever. There was never a period of life before sky. End of story. Nothing more to know. She held the *Big Book* open and pressed the pages to her chest, closed her eyes, and prayed.

THE END

About the Author

Anna B. Moore has published lots of creative nonfiction and a little fiction in places such as *American Scholar, Shenandoah, The Offing, Missouri Review, Pembroke Magazine, Pithead Chapel,* and *Black Warrior Review.* Her essay, "Deathbed," was an honorable mention in Best American Essays 2022. Two others, "That Our Stars Had Become Unmanageable," and "Jenny Dies by Jet Ski," were nominated for Sundress Press Best of the Net Awards in 2022. She lives with her family in Northern California, where she is working on her second novel. Read more of her work at https://www.annabmoore.com/.

About the Press

Unsolicited Press is based out of Portland, Oregon and focuses on the works of the unsung and underrepresented. As a womxn-owned, all-volunteer small publisher that doesn't worry about profits as much as championing exceptional literature, we have the privilege of partnering with authors skirting the fringes of the lit world. We've worked with emerging and award-winning authors such as Frances Daulerio, Shann Ray, Heather Lang-Cassera, Amy Shimshon-Santo, Brook Bhagat, Kris Amos, and John W. Bateman.

Learn more at unsolicitedpress.com. Find us on twitter and instagram.